Dead in Seat 4-A

A Senior Sleuths Mystery

M. Glenda Rosen

Copyright Page

Dead in Seat 4-A
A Senior Sleuths Mystery

First Edition | February 2019
Level Best Books
www.levelbestbooks.com

Trade Paperback ISBN: 978-1-947915-08-4
Also Available in e-book

Printed in the United States of America

Brooke,

For a Mystery Fan,

Marcia

Also by M. Glenda Rosen

(aka Marcia Rosen)

The Senior Sleuth Mysteries:

Dead In Bed
Dead In Seat 4-A

The Dying To Be Beautiful Series:

Without A Head
Fashion Queen
Fake Beauty
Fat Free

Nonfiction:

My Memoir Workbook
The Woman's Business Therapist:
Eliminate the MindBlocks & RoadBlocks to Success

For the women in history I admire who have inspired me to dare to be courageous and continually challenge myself to do more...and to hear their stories from a distance encouraging me to never give up.

And to my family and my dear friends who always make me feel I matter.

Praise for the Senior Sleuths Mysteries

"People who bought *Dead in Bed* from us said they loved it. Clever and funny. We're looking forward to the sequel."

Inquiring Minds, Saugerties, NY
Hudson Valley's Largest Bookstore

"*Dead in Seat 4-A* is filled with suspense, humor, and a great cast of characters. From a key stuffed into a pocket, to a dead body on the plane, we eagerly follow the trail to find out the truth."

Louise Nayer
Author of *Poised for Retirement: Moving from Anxiety to Zen*
and the award winning *Burned: A Memoir*

"I thoroughly enjoyed *Dead in Bed*. I loved the combination of serious crime with humor and zany characters."

Judy Lechner, Author
Death Plays a Solo, A Jazz Mystery

"Marcia Rosen's *Dead in Bed* is fashioned like a Jewish take on the classic *The Thin Man* series, with inspiration from her real-life acquaintance with underworld people like Doc, The Gimp, and others."

Monterey County Weekly

"*Where's the dead guy?* What an opening."

Joyce Olcese, Author,
Mystery Reader Journal: *A Garden Mystery*
The Garden Detective Mysteries

The opening of the second book in The Senior Sleuth Mystery Series is startling. A dead man in the next airplane seat! With crisp dialogue and a strong sense of place (the airplane, Las Vegas), the mystery begins to unfold as Dick and Dora Zimmerman, our senior sleuths, approach a new case of murder with their usual gusto. A joy to read and many fun and funny characters to embrace...particularly Dick and Dora.

Elizabeth Cooke, Author of
Abbi's Forever Home
Abbi's Forever home FOR KIDS

Dead in Seat 4-A draws the reader in right away with the quick pace of the action and the matter-of-fact opening lines. The Senior Sleuths, Dick and Dora, are sporty and smart with no time to waste and lots of action in their lives. M. Glenda Rosen draws the characters with great depth and makes you want to get to know them. She sets the scene and keeps the action moving, so you can hardly wait to find out what is going to happen next.

Betty Withrow, Author of
Prevail: Seven Keys to Create a Personal Victory
The Essential Excuse Handbook

"It's hard to find a mystery that's rollicking good fun and a nail-biter, too, which is why it's great to see Rosen's feisty sleuths and quirky cohorts at it again. There's nothing like cozying up to familiar characters embroiled in new and challenging perils. This time the setting of murder and mayhem is Las Vegas. The seniority factor is hilariously drawn, and the duo continually prove that vitality, creativity, analytic prowess, and deliciously contagious *joie de vivre* transcend age—by a mile!"

Claudia Riess, Author of
Love and Other Hazards

"This second offering of the Senior Sleuths is a hoot—as usual Dora is up to her sleuthing shenanigans and with Las Vegas as a backdrop, what could go wrong? Plenty, and it's great fun."

Marilyn Meredith
Author of *The Deputy Tempe Crabtree Mysteries*

Dead in Seat 4-A

PROLOGUE

Dead Man Flying

T he worn brown leather briefcase fell off his lap, spilling open into the aisle next to Dora.

There were few contents. A flask and an envelope with a key landed next to Dora's seat. The note typed on the envelope only read *Locker 438*.

Leaning over to tell the man in seat 4-A across from her, she gently poked his arm.

No response.

As she pushed harder, the man fell sideways in his seat.

"Dick, wake up, I think the man across from me is dead."

"Dora, leave the man alone."

"Dear, I said he's dead."

Without much thought, Dora picked up the envelope and key and slipped it into her jacket pocket.

The Zimmermans

H ere I am again. It's me, Dora Zimmerman. Remember? I've told you about my husband, the handsome, irascible and incredibly charming Dick Zimmerman.

We are on our way to Las Vegas after being involved in a murder case in Manhattan where there were numerous dead bodies, several attempts on our lives, and interesting conversations with a lovely, elderly neighbor who had been a star in noir films of the 1940s and 50s.

He wants to do a movie about us.

No way!

Anyhow, we're retired and can afford the luxury of flying first class. So we do. Why not?

Our long-time friend and sleuthing buddy, Zero the Bookie, hates to fly and has rented a car to drive to meet us in Vegas.

We are done with murders and crime. Maybe.

We have interesting friends like Frankie Socks, who we left in New York. Once in the Witness Protection Program, he refuses to ever leave Manhattan again. He likes to keep an eye on us. Dick had kept in touch with him and told him when it had finally been safe at last to "come back home."

In Las Vegas, Buzz takes up the slack for Frankie. He's a tough guy with a soft heart. But it's best not to cross him.

Our condo in Manhattan's Skyline Vista is known as The Mansion.

In Vegas, our other home is located in the Desert View Condo Complex, and is known as The Star.

Yes, there is a story there too. More on that later.

The sheriff in Vegas is never unhappy when we are back east. He thinks we attract trouble to his town. That's possible. In the past there were some incidents. Okay, murders. But he agrees we did help solve those cases.

We can't help ourselves. It's in our DNA.

Dick and I have been married for forty years. He used to be a criminal defense attorney. He stood up for a lot of good guys, but also some bad guys.

I was a lawyer, then a judge in divorce court. I know I've said this before, but there were some criminals in there that were worse than murderers. Men and women who were abusive or caused pain to their parters or their children, who hid money so they didn't have to pay alimony or child support. They would sometimes fight in court. It was like being in a boxing ring and I was the referee.

Vegas has grown by leaps and bounds over the last half-century, from a Mob haven to what it is today with millions of visitors each year, some hoping it will be the place where their dreams for big money come true.

It's a gambling town in the middle of the desert. For miles in every direction, well past the highrise hotels with flashing neon signs begging visitors to take their chances at their casinos, is a wide expanse of arid land boasting 100-plus degree summers.

Dick and I, and Zero too, prefer to spend the cold Manhattan winter months in Las Vegas.

We see our two grown sons and their families a few times a year. They love us. From a distance. They think we get into too much trouble.

Last year, a Manhattan medical examiner friend of mine suggested I write about our crime adventures. So, I thought, why not?

Well, here's another story. The first one, *Dead in Bed*, was exciting. Well, except for when the bad guys tried to kill us.

This particular drama began at over forty thousand feet in the air.

Murder, shady dealings, shadier characters, suspense, deceit, romantic flings and a surprise or two awaited us in Vegas.

By the way, I do love Dick to death.

Chapter One

Seat 4-A

"Where's the dead guy?"

Sheriff Brady Foster, his voice raspy from years of smoking unfiltered cigarettes, stood at the steps to the bottom of the plane as coach passengers traipsed off like sheep heading to gamble, party and maybe even get married in an Elvis-style chapel. The county coroner medical examiner and a forensics team were right behind the sheriff waiting to get on the plane.

Foster, a Vegas old timer, and sheriff for almost forty years, was tall and lean with short grey hair usually covered with an LVPD tan baseball cap. Agitated and cranky, he climbed aboard the plane that landed in *his* city with a dead body.

Dick was slumped down in his seat pretending to be asleep.

"Tell your husband I know he's faking sleep. Again, the two of you with another dead body. It's enough to ban you from my city."

Before Dora could say anything, Foster turned away and walked over to the medical examiner who was checking on the dead man.

"Rigor mortis has set in. He's been dead several hours, Sheriff. I'll tell you more after the autopsy."

The pilot, co-pilot, two flight attendants and four first class passengers plus the Zimmermans waited to be questioned after the body was loaded onto a gurney, covered and taken off the plane. The Clark County Coroner and Medical Examiner's Office was located in a desert-colored stucco building where, surprisingly, trees and bushes grew around the perimeter. This is where deaths under suspicious circumstances were examined for cause, and those victims unidentified would be added to the National Missing and Unidentified Persons System, or NamUS.

Over the years, Vegas had been host to numerous murders by the Mob. The criminal underworld had invaded the city, ran its gambling operations and used fear as its motivating force. Much of the city had been run by organized crime, crooked politicians, and law enforcement on their payroll. The wise guys as they were known, flaunted their money

Sheriff Brady Foster had dealt with all of these types at one time or another, although finding a dead body on a plane was a new one for him. "Most murders are for money, love and hate, and of course, revenge," he had once told a group of police cadets visiting his department and power. "Certainly there are those who enjoy being vicious and cruel to please their own distorted image of life, of right and wrong."

Gathered in the first class section of the plane he shouted over various noises, "I want to know what each of you were doing and if you saw anything."

The pilot glared. "Sheriff, I assume you're aware

the co-pilot and I were flying this damn plane and the crew was taking care of passengers."

Ignoring his comment Brady shouted, "Was anyone on the plane talking to him?"

Everyone shook their heads.

"Dick, stop giving me that look," Dora said.

"You couldn't let him alone and watch him sleep, dear?"

"Darling, he wasn't asleep. He was dead."

"One of the crew could have discovered him after we were off the plane."

"And us miss all this excitement?"

Dora was grinning. Dick was silent.

"I've texted Buzz to wait inside the airport for us," Dick sat back, obviously not happy with Dora for once again getting them involved with a dead body.

"Have you heard from Zero? Has he arrived yet?"

"No."

"Just no? What gives?" Dora inched closer, intrigued.

"He told me he was stopping in Albuquerque on his way westward."

"Good grief, why? Isn't there enough desert in Vegas for him?"

"He stopped to see someone."

"Who?" Now Dora was really curious. "Look at me."

"Dear, I really don't know."

Dick had been watching the police activity outside as crime scene tape was being stretched across the tarmac at McCarran Airport. The plane would be required to sit parked for several days, making for an unhappy airport and airline. Police cars were parked nearby and passengers and people waiting for departures and arrivals were in the terminal staring out at a scene that could have been in a movie. It was controlled chaos. None of which deterred Dora from wanting to know what was going on with Zero.

"Dick, don't make me cause a fuss. You do know what Zero's up to, don't you?"

"Would you really embarrass the love of your life?"

"Absolutely." Leaning back in her seat, 4-C, eyes closed, Dora knew he would eventually give in to her questioning...and charms.

"Fine. He's visiting someone he met on an internet gambling site."

"You're kidding! Our Zero has a date with someone in the middle of nowhere?"

"It's a big city, sort of. It has good Mexican food." Dick couldn't help laughing.

"Who is she?"

"Wouldn't tell me."

"What if she's an axe murderer?"

"Guess he won't show up in Vegas."

"Dick, please call him. Never mind, I will." Dora reached in her white leather tote bag for her cell phone while Dick attempted to charm the local constabulary, who knew him all too well.

"Nice to see you, Sheriff." Dick grinned. The sheriff stared at him, as if daring him to say another word.

After over an hour of crew and passengers being questioned, the sheriff told Deputy Greg Turner to arrange a time for everyone to be at the station the next afternoon and to schedule the Zimmermans last.

"Yes sir?" Turner said, raising his eyebrows at the

Zimmermans. He knew them well. He had done some private investigating for them in the past.

That's another story for another day.

In the meantime, Dora noticed the sheriff took the victim's brief case and envelope with him. For the moment Dora forgot she had the dead man's key she found on the floor of the plane.

Or did she?

With that the sheriff stomped off the plane, got into his police car, turned on his siren, and followed the medical examiner out of the airport. The forensic team would remain on the plane going through the victim's seat, other seats and the aisles in first class, long after everyone departed. They would also take the dead man's flask and examine what was in it.

Crime seemed to find Dick and Dora Zimmerman. Old friends asked for help, new friends sought their guidance, the police sometimes requested their assistance, and it seemed murder fell into their laps.

Then, there were the criminals who attempted to shut them up.

Wherever they lived there were two photos of them side-by-side. One from when they first met, young, carefree, and good looking. The later one taken when they recently celebrated their fortieth anniversary. Older, but still both carefree and good looking.

Dick was handsome with dark green eyes, his full head of hair gray except for a few black streaks of his youth remaining. He was dressed in an Armani tuxedo. Dora was elegant and attractive, her dark brown hair shoulder-length and thanks to her gene pool, she was still slender. In their anniversary photo she was wearing a deep blue satin designer gown the color of her eyes.

Like everyone, their lives had disappointments and hurts, however, they preferred not to dwell on them. They were grateful for the good things.

The center of their lives' work had always involved justice, and even in retirement Dora found solving crimes exciting and challenging. Dick preferred poker, the ponies and partying. Still, Dora managed to push him into helping solve any crime that came their way.

He would say, "No, absolutely no way."

Dora would give him a hug, a kiss on the cheek or put her arm through his, knowing she could charm him into saying, "Maybe."

Once he said maybe, she knew she had him. He knew it too.

Dick would catch Zero laughing at these exchanges, raise his eyebrows and promise him, "Don't think you're not getting involved too."

The death of the man in seat 4-A would be declared a murder and it was only the beginning of a mystery that would push Dick and Dora, along with Zero and others into dangerous situations where they would soon find old friends were not what they seemed to be.

Neither were the new ones.

Then, there was the key.

A few years earlier a New York City reporter and poker buddy of Dick's wrote a front-page story about Dick and Dora's involvement in the capture of a couple of murderers in which he called them "The Senior Sleuths."

Dora loved it. Dick not so much.

Chapter Two

Our Senior Sleuths

D ora listened to the responses as the sheriff questioned the four other first class passengers.

The couple seated three rows behind her and Dick were clearly heading for big spending in Vegas. Maybe in their fifties, they wore fashionable clothes, their overhead luggage, pulled down by a flight attendant, was Louis Vuitton and each wore plenty of gaudy, albeit expensive, jewelry.

Across the aisle were two attractive men, perhaps in their thirties, holding hands.

Dora noticed that the co-pilot and one of the first class flight attendants, an attractive red head, kept glancing at each other.

"Dick, see those two?"

Turning away from the action outside the plane, he asked, "What?"

"The co-pilot and the flight attendant?"

"Yes dear, I see them…and your point is?"

"I think there's something going on between them."

"You think they conspired to get rid of one of the passengers?"

"Oh good grief, no. Well, who knows, maybe, and he's at least twenty-five years older than her."

"Love's a beautiful thing," Dick said wryly.

"It's probably more like lust."

"Dora, stop. The sheriff will figure out what happened to him without our help."

Sitting back in their comfortable first class seats, with double the legroom of coach, the scene outside was a reminder of their friend in New York who had starred in a number of old black and white noir films. Now in his nineties and still spry, they had drinks with him a few nights before leaving for Vegas.

"I'm going to make a few phone calls," he told them. "Someone should make a movie about you two."

"Don't you dare," Dick reminded him, "I'm a lawyer. I'll sue. Plus it's an absurd idea."

"What do you think, my dear?"

Dora burst out laughing. "Please. Those old noir films were about tough, hard drinking detectives, smoking cigarettes. And about good looking, dangerous blondes they called broads or dames, or even gun molls."

"You don't think you qualify for that distinction?"

"No way. And Dick wouldn't ever call me any of those names. Would you, dear?"

"Certainly not."

Getting up, Dora gave their new friend the famous film star a kiss on the cheek and they left, promising to stay in touch.

Chapter Three

Old Vegas

Sheriff Foster knew about old time Vegas.

A young man when he started on the police force, he had occasion to come in contact with some of the mobsters who ran the Vegas hotels and casinos.

At dinner one night a couple years earlier, with the Zimms, (which was what people sometimes called the Zimmermans), Zero, and a few other friends, the talk was about the *not* so good old days.

"I'll bet there were plenty of bodies found in those days."

"Zero, you'll bet on anything," Dora said, giving him a loving punch.

"Yeah, well I bet this town was something back in the day."

Foster sat back holding the last of his drink. "Old timers will tell you it felt like the Wild West. You should visit The Mob Museum. They have photos and backgrounds on most of the major players, although there certainly is nothing about them to glorify. Most were murderers many times over like Bugsy Segal who built the Flamingo Hotel on the Strip. Of course, there was Meyer Lansky, Lucky Luciano, and eventually Al Capone. They all had two things in common: A deep desire for power, and a willingness to be violent and ruthless to get it." Dick motioned for the waiter to bring them another round of drinks. No one was quite ready to leave. The atmosphere inside this popular local bar and restaurant was cozy and the conversation about what Vegas once was continued to be intriguing.

Foster reminded them, "Many of the films and books about the Mob glamorized these characters, made them seem human because they protected their own families. Truth is they were violent and committed brutal murders."

"What about the downtown district? Old Las Vegas pretty much centered around that area didn't it?" Dora kicked Zero under the table. He had been busy checking out the shapely brunette at the bar while pretending to listen to the sheriff.

"Lots of gambling and chaos took place on Fremont Street. After the Mob rule ended it was run-down for a while. Then some investors brought it back to life. It's a fun change from the Strip."

"How did the police finally clean up the Mob rule?" asked Dora.

"Many were killed, some went to jail, others died of old age. But most importantly, the state created tighter regulations for casino ownership."

Dick finished his drink and paid the check. "Now there are too many casinos, so much glitz and flash and year-in-year-out, people who come here, hoping to beat the odds and become the next big winner."

"You mean like your buddy Zero here?"

That got his attention. "Huh, me, what?"

Chapter Four

Buzz

While waiting to pick up Dick and Dora at McCarran Airport in Vegas, Buzz tossed a hundred bucks into the slots. Like Zero, he loved to gamble. And also like Dick, he enjoyed drinking.

He would also pick them up the next afternoon to go to the police station, all of these rides taken in his turquoise and white pristine condition, '56 Chevy Convertible.

"Traffic is terrible. Couple big conventions in town. What happened on the plane, Boss?"

"I'm not your boss," said Dick.

"I know, but I like calling you that. It interests people."

"You two stop it. People are driving like lunatics. Just get me home," said Dora.

"Need a drink, darling?"

"Yes, Dick, I need a drink, a shower and to forget about dead bodies for now."

"Your fault," he said.

"Dora, did you kill someone on the plane?" Buzz burst out laughing as he was maneuvering through traffic.

"What? Of course not."

"My lovely wife discovered a dead body in the seat across from her. Bless her heart, she can't mind her own business."

Buzz wasn't sure what was going on. He had been in a dark airport waiting area by the slot machines, and now they were on the darkening evening streets of Vegas. The city was filled with tourists, couples with young kids, teens half-dressed and gamblers dreaming of winning a big jackpot.

"I'll take back roads to The Star to get away from this traffic. There's also a big show tonight at The Mirage."

The exhausted Zimms were quiet and dozing, still on east coast time.

Other than his buzzard-shaped nose, Buzz was a good-looking guy who kept watch over the Zimmermans when they were in Vegas. He liked them. They had been good to him, giving him work when he was down and out because of his gambling habit. His services included some transportation, setting up poker games and making use of his extensive personal connections. With the Zimmermans' penchant for getting involved in murders and other sordid criminal activities, those connections were extremely helpful and valuable.

Leaning over the front seat Dora asked, "Buzz, can you check with your buddies to find out how much the sheriff knows about the dead man on the plane?"

"Sure thing. By the way, is Zero coming to Vegas soon?"

That started Dora off into a tirade, shouting, "Can you believe it? He's bringing a woman with him. Good grief, he met her on an internet gambling site."

"Seriously?"

"Don't get her started. We'll meet the lady soon enough." Dick yawned, his head shaking no, his eyes begging Buzz to not talk about it anymore.

Pulling into the condo garage, Buzz told them, "I called management earlier today. They've got your condo air conditioner going and had a couple days' worth of food delivered."

"You're a treasure, my good man. Please pick us up at half past four tomorrow afternoon. We have to be at the sheriff's at five."

"Will do.

"By the way, anything exciting happening here other than the usual Vegas chaos?" Dick was halfway out the door when he heard Buzz say, "Well..."

"Well what? Please tell me no one has been found dead at The Star," said Dora sliding across the back seat to follow Dick.

"Not there."

Dick took her hand. "Darling, we'll find out tomorrow about the other lovely happenings in Sin City."

Dora hesitated. "One question. Where and when did they find a dead body?"

"That's two questions," said Buzz.

"Answer me." Dora refused to move completely out of the car.

"In the desert. Like old time Vegas. They found a dead body yesterday. And before you ask, I have no idea who it is."

Buzz got out of the car, unlatched the trunk, collected their luggage and went upstairs with the weary couple. "I'll see you tomorrow, Boss. Call if you need me before then." Smirking, he added, "By the way, what is that on your face?"

Dick glared at him without commenting. Dora grinned. He had grown a mustache and was far from the end of his being teased about it.

After Buzz left, he headed to a nightspot where his pals hung out and various criminal elements could find each other. The kind of place where talk of recent murders would be discussed. Maybe even planned.

It was nearly midnight by the time Buzz got there. He sat at the far end of the bar, ordered a beer and before looking up at the television took notice of two men sitting in a back booth. This was not the first time he had seen them there, whispering, cautiously glancing around...nor would it be the last.

When he set down his beer, Buzz asked the bartender, "Hey know those two guys over there?"

"Nah."

Buzz was sure he was lying. He had a tell. He would start wiping the bar counter. Back and forth. Back and forth.

Chapter Five

Zero...On the Road Again

He had driven through Albuquerque, New Mexico a dozen times. Sometimes he stayed overnight, but more often he kept going west to California to visit friends, then headed back east to Vegas.

Dick once remarked to Zero, "You do know it's a bit out of the way going to California before coming to Las Vegas."

"Cute, sarcasm does not look good on you. Yes, I know. But I like driving, hate flying."

Central Avenue ran through the heart of the city that had been part of the famous Route 66. Written about by Jack Kerouac in *On the Road* and even on the television series *77 Sunset Strip*, this area brought memories both good and bad to those who had lived on it or travelled over it in the mid-twentieth century.

The city it ran through was once known for having more fast food restaurants than any other city its size. One of its main charms, to those who lived on this dry landscape was the Sandia Mountains and the frequent multi-color sunsets. But the city could feel hard, unwelcoming. It was Indian land, stolen from them, and some people said you could still feel their presence. New Mexico was also home to Los Alamos, where the atom bomb was built and tested. What evil remains is hard to know. Zero had heard Dora's call. He ignored it. For now.

"Zero, where are you? Call me. I need to know you're okay. Can you believe there was a dead body on the plane across from my seat?"

Zero smiled, thinking *Yes I can.*

Later, Dora tried again. "Zero, should we call the police?"

After midnight Vegas time, Zero finally called his childhood friend.

"Hey, Lady D. All is fine. You'll tell me about the dead body soon enough. We'll be there tomorrow."

"Excuse me? We'll? What does that mean?"

"It means we will. Ta ta love." Click.

Dora huffed, "Dick, he's bringing some woman he just met."

"Oh, good for him."

"Good? Are you nuts?"

"He should have a love life."

"You're impossible."

"I'm going to bed. It's two a.m., which means it's five in the morning New York time. Thanks to you my love, we're expected at the sheriff's office this afternoon and I need my beauty sleep."

With that, Dora threw a pillow at him, then checked her phone and saw that Zero had emailed them.

Attached was a photo of an attractive woman, maybe in her early fifties. The subject line read *Meet Cloud.*

Cloud appeared to be Native American, with long dark hair and piercing black eyes.

Turning off the lights as Vegas continued to face

its world of shadowy excesses, Dora wondered about Cloud's story.

As flashing neon lights lured gamblers to their casinos, Dora punched her pillow into place harder than usual, mumbling, "What are those two up to?"

Dick was sound asleep. Or, once again pretending to be asleep.

"I know you're awake. After forty years, my love, I know your sleep noises."

With that Dick gave out a loud snore, knowing there was plenty of time for them to find out about the steamy stories, murder and romance.

Dora would be sure of that.

Chapter Six

Dame Isabella Grayson

For over twenty years, her beautiful face, long red hair, blue eyes and French accent had captured the hearts of men and spurred the jealousy of women as she made love on the big screen to many of Hollywood's leading men. Being tall and lean increased her box office appeal. The "Dame" in front of her name was the invention of the studio publicity department meant to create a sense of mystery about her.

Age had not been kind to her, thanks to years of three-martini-a-day lunches and then two large evening cocktails. At eighty-seven, the beauty of her youth had faded many years earlier.

Her earnings, wisely invested by her ex-husband and manager, allowed her to live at The Star in Las Vegas. Dame Isabella Grayson told anyone who would listen, "My crush is on Zero Zimmerman. He will soon be mine."

She had once said to Zero, "I adore you. Why won't you make love to me?"

The first time it happened, Zero laughed, thinking she was joking. She was not, so he apologized, gave her a kiss on a heavily rouged cheek and walked away.

"See, he kiss me. He want me."

Wearing billowy satin slacks, long sleeve silk or satin tops, and a great deal of jewelry, including rings, dangling earrings, necklaces and half a dozen bracelets, she loved attention, especially Zero's.

Banging on the Zimms' door at eight in the morning, Dame Isabella demanded in her French accent, "Where my Zero is? Why he not come here with you? I not leave until I know."

Groggy, having only had a few hours sleep, Dick shouted through the closed door, "He'll be here in a few days. Go away, we're sleeping."

"You tell him, I wait for him." Her satin slacks, too long on her increasingly frail body, moved across the hall floor. Dick went back to bed, leaving Dora laughing.

"Not funny, my love. She's a pain."

"Yes, but she's crazy about our Zero."

"She's crazy, plain and simple. And so are you if you don't go back to sleep," Dick said grumpily.

"I have a wonderful idea."

"I'm hoping it's about sleeping."

"You and Zero should go on a double date with your older lady loves."

Dick turned and glared at Dora. "What are you talking about?"

"In New York, Bertie Gladstone is in love with you. See how perfect it would be for both you and Zero?"

Bertie Gladstone, eighty-nine-years-young as she described herself, each day put on make-up, fixed her bleached-blond hair, and dressed up with colorful clothes and jewelry to match. Ready to face her public, off she went with her walker, a gift from having had a slight stroke. Her best feature was her sense of humor.

Living in the same condo as the Zimms, The Mansion, in New York City, she had helped them catch, well at least slow down, the escape of a couple of murderers before coming to Las Vegas.

Bertie was a flirt and had a big crush on Dick. When asked why she dressed so fancy every day, Bertie responded, "I'm looking for my fourth husband." She meant it.

"Dora, turn off the light. What are you doing?"

"I'm emailing Zero about plans for you guys to double date."

Dick walked over, took away her phone, turned off the light, and well, the rest is personal.

Chapter Seven

Vegas Law

Las Vegas Metropolitan Sheriff Brady Foster was born and raised in the desert town and knew plenty about casinos, gamblers and bodies buried during the height of the Mob days. Once quoted in a local paper, he said, "Sure, casinos have staff watching over their operations but disappointments and frustrations spill out onto the city streets. My police department has their hands full, and they keep their guns loaded."

His chief deputy, Greg Turner, who was in his mid-thirties and slightly shorter, was easily recognized around town by his red hair, charming smile, and muscles bulging beneath a tight t-shirt when off duty. Body builder turned police officer, he was the perfect complement to the gruff-acting sheriff.

Foster said, "Keeps suspects on their toes. They figure I might arrest them just to be mean."

Turner had laughed. Originally from the south he spoke with a slow drawl and had a southern charm he used to his advantage, at work and in romance. He admitted with a huge smile, "I love the ladies and they seem to love me."

Vegas law enforcement personnel had increased

significantly as did advances in technologies. Dealing with gamblers, disgruntled losers and celebratory winners twenty-four hours a day meant plenty of problems.

By the time Dick and Dora arrived at the police station, the pilots, crew and other first class passengers had been interviewed and there seemed to be no concern about them being involved in the death of the man in seat 4-A.

It was late afternoon and the desert air had begun to cool. However, the sheriff's mood had not improved. He grumbled to Turner as the Zimms came into the station, "Those two make me crazy. Bring them into the conference room and stay with us. I might want to throw them in jail."

Turner ignored the sheriff's comments. He knew the gruffness meant nothing. The sheriff not only liked the Zimmermans, he often played poker with Dick and his buddies.

The sheriff asked, "Dora, did you know the guy in seat 4-A?"

"What? No."

"Dick, you?"

"Me, what?"

"Did you know the dead guy?"

"Don't think so," said Dick.

"How did you know he was dead?"

"Dora, dearest," Dick said sarcastically, "tell the sheriff how you knew he was dead."

"Okay you two stop this game of cat and mouse." The sheriff wasn't amused.

Dora said, "I tried talking to him a couple times, then sort of noticed he wasn't breathing."

"Sort of noticed?"

"Yes."

"How did you sort of notice?"

"His briefcase fell on the floor, I poked him gently in the arm to tell him and he didn't respond," Dora replied.

"Then what happened?"

"He fell over in his seat and I suggested to Dick the man was dead."

Dick stood up, pushing his chair in under the table. "Come on, Brady, enough of this. You've known Dora and me for years. We didn't murder anyone and we have no idea who killed this guy. Who was he and what killed him?"

Taking off his hat, Sheriff Foster set it on the table, and then turned over several photos of the murdered man with a sigh of resignation. "Poison."

"What kind?"

Passing a report to them the sheriff said, "A good old Agatha Christie standby. Arsenic. It was in the flask he brought on board with him. Don't look at me like that, I do read you know."

Dick picked up one of the photos, "There's an inscription on the flask."

"Yeah it says *With love, Jane.*"

"So who's Jane?"

"His wife."

"Does she know?"

"We reached her a couple hours ago and found out she was waiting for him here in Vegas. She'll be in to identify the body in the morning and we'll talk to her then."

"Who is the dead man?" Dick still held the photos.

"Zachary Kohl, a chunky, bald, middle-aged man wearing a thousand dollar suit, a huge diamond pinky ring and carrying the deadly flask in his briefcase along with an envelope. He had only a few hundred dollars in his wallet."

The four of them stared at the photos of the dead man, spread out on the large round table. Dora took the photos from Dick and after staring closely at them, said, "Brady, I think there was a news story about him a couple weeks ago."

"For what?"

"I didn't pay much attention to it."

Foster nodded to his deputy. Ten minutes later Turner came in with a printout of the story in a New York paper and said, "Kohl was being accused of money laundering. It's vague. Doesn't say for who."

Dora replied, "You probably couldn't recognize him on the plane. He was wearing huge sunglasses and a hairpiece. He probably began to feel sick even before he got on the plane, hoping to get to Vegas and take care of whatever ailed him."

"Yeah except what ailed him was permanent," commented Dora.

The sheriff replied, "Someone had to tamper with that flask before he got on the plane."

Dora stood and started to stuff the police report in her bag. "We really need to go, Sheriff."

"Oh no you don't. Give me that report."

She held it away from him. "I will," she said offering her most charming smile "But, first tell us about the body found in the desert. Any connection to Zachary Kohl being murdered?"

Grabbing the report from Dora, Dick handed it to the sheriff. "Call us when you have it all figured out."

Sheriff Foster began rubbing his forehead as he

turned to his deputy. "I really should throw them in jail. You know they're going to try and investigate this murder."

If only he could stop them.

Dick and Dora were bound to get involved. Seriously and possibly deadly involved.

After they left the sheriff shook his head remarking to his deputy, "That mustache makes him look like a crook."

"Let's stop for something to eat, I'm starved." Dora sat back in deep thought.

Dick said, "Buzz, you heard the lady, go to the burger place we like over in Summerlin."

Once there, pulling Buzz aside, Dora told him, "Tomorrow, eleven a.m., I need you to take me somewhere. Alone."

Chapter Eight

The Star

The neon lights of hotels and casinos on the Strip could be seen miles away from the Zimmermans' living room window and balcony. The balcony was often too hot to enjoy for more than a few minutes during the day, but sometimes with the cool desert breeze at night, it was pleasant enough to end the day looking up at the moon and stars shining bright like the Vegas neon signs.

With a stop for burgers and drinks at a restaurant far from the madding crowd, Buzz and the Zimmermans discussed, what else, murder.

"Boss, I checked, no details on the murders, so far," said Buzz.

"They'll need to do autopsies," Dora announced.

"Darling, we do know that."

The bar had filled with people who knew to stay away from the madness of the Strip at night. The booths and bar stools were black, the counters and tables, black and red checkered. An old jukebox was in the corner, silent for many years.

"Dick, my dear, what are *we* going to do about the murders?"

Buzz looked up, grinned and quietly went back to

enjoying his burger and draft beer.

"Dora, *we* are going to let the sheriff do his job while we enjoy time with friends and relax."

"Well, I found the body on the plane. Can't ignore it."

"I'm trying to, if only you'll let me."

The news came on the television over the bar and a newscaster reported that an unidentified body had been found in the desert. Dick and Dora listened in silence. At almost the same time, Dora's cell phone rang.

"Hey darling, it's Zero. We're well on our way to Vegas. Plan for dinner for four tomorrow night at the Black Tie Steak House. Bye, love." He clicked off again before Dora could even answer him. She knew he'd hung up on purpose.

After the check was settled, Buzz went out and brought the car around. He wanted to find out more about the murder plus he had plans to hang out again with some of his pals. Pals, who like him, had a history in Vegas that would prove more than a little helpful in the near future.

Buzz grinned. "Give it up, Boss. You know she'll convince you to get involved."

"Damn him," said Dora.

"Who?"

Dora relayed Zero's message, then told Dick, "I'll make reservations. I want to have a word or two with him after we meet this Cloud person."

"By the way, you two," Buzz seemed to suddenly remember, "I heard another celebrity has moved into The Star. Someone who is scheduled for six months at one of the casinos on the Strip. I'm not sure who. Not yet."

Dick shrugged. "No wonder the place got its name for putting up with these stars and their behavior. Remember the time one of them tried to dive into the pool from his balcony?"

"Only broke his legs, Boss."

"Lucky he didn't break his neck. Probably because he only jumped from the second floor."

"Oh I think my husband's favorite was the model parading around the property nude for a few nights." Dora smiled and poked Dick in the arm.

"Yes, dear. Sorry she had to move away," he said drily

"Buzz, please look into the murders. Get some information from your contacts, whoever they are."

Nodding his head, he pulled in front of The Star and said goodnight. He was off to try and figure out whatever Mrs. Z. wanted. He had a bad feeling he was going to need help from his friends. Some were a little seedy, some a little unsavory, some downright criminals who knew about the places and people who made up the underworld of Vegas. Maybe these people were not the old time Mafia or "made men" of organized crime, but there were still enough bad deeds done that were worthy of attention. His pals knew plenty of gossip and could be counted on. Buzz was, in many ways, one of them. They had also been able to count on him.

No matter if people believed it or not, an element of underworld life still existed. Leave it to Las Vegas to have the Mob Museum and even fascinating tours about the Mob world and the often fascinating and outrageous mobsters who were once prominent in the city.

The night before, Buzz was greeted by his pals with respect, one who belonged, who knew his way around. Behind the bar, the owner wearing a black shirt and black apron, called to Buzz's favorite waitress to bring him his regular draft beer.

"Thought you had to pick up your boss today," she said.

"I did. He and the wife are home. They were delayed because of a murder on the plane. A man was found dead across from them."

"And they're involved?"

Buzz nodded. "I told them I would see what I could find out. Have you heard anything about it?"

"Not a thing. Give it a couple of nights."

Buzz who noticed the bartender was listening while trying to appear nonchalant, nodded. A few minutes later he finished his beer and left. The waitress was done for the night and waited for him outside.

The Underworld Saloon was well known, having been a popular spot for years. It was frequented by those seeking to drink and scheme at the edges of the bright lights of the city. Nearly every place has a spot like the Underworld, dark, inhabited by lost souls, schemers and scammers, a place where secrets are guarded. The people who work in places like that make it a point to look the other way during their patrons' conversations.

The Underworld Saloon had a long bar on the left with blood red cracked leather bar stools patrons could sit on for as long as they wanted, as long as they kept drinking. On the wall were black-and-white photos of infamous mobsters interspersed with film posters from *The Godfather, Scarface, Goodfellas,* and *Chinatown,* and older movies including *The Maltese Falcon, Laura, Double*

Indemnity, Out of the Past.

Once a year the bar held a look-alike contest for the regulars. The men would come decked out in raincoats and fedoras, while the ladies donned bleached blonde wigs, and tight-fitting dresses and come hither eyes, trying their best to emulate the famous femme fatale movie stars of the big screen.

The Underworld was a place plans could be made, Buzz thought, as he walked to his car, arm around his lady friend.

"I'd better be sure to have some backup ready. I have no idea what the boss and his wife are likely to do next."

How right he was.

Chapter Nine

The Key

"Go to the bus station."

"What?"

"Buzz, take me to the bus station. It's over on Main Street near downtown."

"Mrs. Z, it's not the best place for you to go. It's not always the best element of people hanging out there."

"I'll be safe. You're with me."

"I'll only take you if you tell me what this is about."

He stopped the car on the side of the road, and waited for an answer.

"I found a key on the airplane," Dora said with a sigh. "Actually, it fell out of the dead man's briefcase. I picked it up and forgot to give it to the sheriff. I figured we might as well check it out ourselves first."

"What? When the sheriff finds out you kept something of the dead man's he'll lock you up for the rest of your life."

"You're exaggerating."

"Dora, trust me, the sheriff has a mean streak a mile long and if I help you this puts us both in the middle of it. You know he'll go nuts when he finds this out."

"Okay, drop me off. I'll go alone." Dora grinned opening the car door.

"Fine. Let's go. Close the door." Sighing, Buzz started up the car and drove them toward what he was sure was trouble.

The Las Vegas bus station was the preferred travel choice for many elderly people with limited incomes, those who wanted to see the landscape of America from the ground, as well as runaway kids.

The key Dora picked up was for locker 438, which was in the second row from the end on the right. Dozens of people were in the terminal, arriving, waiting to leave, or just hanging out. Buzz watched curiously as Dora opened the locker.

No one seemed to notice them at the lockers. Still, Buzz didn't like what was happening, not at all, and whether Mrs. Z. liked it or not, they were going to the police station from here. Pulling out a large manila envelope, Dora dropped it in her bag, and together they walked quickly back to the car, and left the terminal. When she noticed where he was heading, she said, "First at least let me see what's in this envelope."

Sitting back, opening it up, Dora sat stunned.

"Buzz, you're right, get to the police station. I'll happily settle for screaming from the sheriff. Oh, and call Dick to meet us there."

At the police station, Foster carefully opened the envelope.

Inside was a gun with the serial number scratched

off, twenty-five thousand dollars in cash, and a photo accompanied by a note. Instructions about a hit that Kohl, the dead man on the plane, had been hired for.

Even Foster, who had seen a lot of strange, unsettling things over his years in law enforcement, was stunned as he eyed the photo. He tasked a deputy to check out the locker, handing him the key, and giving Dora a dirty look. "Find out who rented this locker and when. Get a warrant from one of the judges so we haven't any problems with opening it."

Dick joined Dora and Buzz. Furious, he sat in one of the police interrogation rooms unwilling to discuss anything about the key. He was staring at his wife who was for the moment not willing to look back at him. There was the sheriff to deal with first.

"How did you get the key and why the hell didn't you give it to me right away?" Sheriff Foster was shouting, pointing at her, downright furious.

"Can I plead the Fifth Amendment?" Dora was attempting, rather unsuccessfully, to lighten the mood "You can plead insanity for all I care. Stay here until I know what this is all about."

Dora finally dared to look at her husband, who got up and whispered in her ear. "Darling, I want a divorce."

Dora couldn't help but laugh. Dick always said that when he was furious with something she'd done. He never meant it, of course.

Dick and Dora Zimmerman sat quietly until, almost an hour later, Deputy Turner called. "You won't believe this. The bus locker was paid for last week by Zachary Kohl."

Chapter Ten

Iced

L ess than fifty miles outside the city limits of Vegas, away from the famous Strip, two college boys high on weed and booze saw a refrigerator in the desert about a quarter mile off the main road.

It was well after midnight and they had pulled over to use the desert as a bathroom facility. At night the desert silence was interrupted by the sounds of scurrying rabbits, coyotes, ground squirrels, even an eagle or hawk. They made sure not to step on a desert tortoise or snake.

Many bodies had been buried out in the desert when the Mob ruled Las Vegas. Those caught cheating were either found dead or never seen again. And sometimes those caught being a rats or stool pigeons were beaten, murdered and buried under the unrelenting desert sun.

What the stoned college boys found was an icebox, the kind used in homes a hundred years earlier. It was obviously a strange thing to see on this desert road, the questions became how did it get there and by who. But, even more so, why?

"Pull it open."

"You do it."

"What does the note on it say?"

"Don't open. Contents are rotten."

"I'm calling the cops."

"We'll be arrested if they catch us here with all the weed and booze in the car."

"Shit. You're right."

"I'm always right."

"You're always full of it."

The night sounds seemed louder to a couple stoned college boys, used to city life and city comforts.

"Hey man, let's get out of here. It's kinda creepy."

"Yeah, there's a weird smell coming from it."

"Let's get back to school and call the cops from there."

"Good thinking, Sherlock."

Three hours later, after receiving the call, the sergeant on duty sent two deputies out to see what the fuss was about. It was late morning when they left and the day was heating up, even more so in the open desert.

"Probably just a college prank."

"Still better to check it out."

"Callers said there's a note on it."

"Great, more nonsense."

"If the college boys are pulling a prank we should arrest their sorry asses. All that money on tuition and this is all they have to do is send us on a wild goose chase."

Once off the Strip away from traffic, the ride out beyond the city took little time and they spotted the ice-box sitting out in the desert.

"Damn, not exactly something one usually finds in the desert, or anywhere else for that matter in this day and age."

Pulling off to the side of the road, walking the distance into the desert, putting on gloves, one deputy took the note off the front of the icebox, the other pulled the door to open it.

"The smell is awful."

The officers covered their faces with their shirtsleeves and did their best not to give their breakfast over to the desert as they gagged.

"The note did say the contents are rotten."

"I'll be damned. There's a body inside."

"What the hell. How did this get here? Better call the station, tell Sheriff Foster."

"Sir, we're by the refrigerator call that came in earlier," the officer said into his phone. "It's an old fashioned ice box."

"So?"

"So, there's a dead body inside and another note on it. Looks like a female victim."

"I'll get the coroner and forensics out there as soon as possible. Wait for them."

"Tell them to bring some Vicks for the smell. It's sickening."

"What does the note on the body say?"

"Rotten to the core."

Sheriff Foster, sitting at his desk messy with papers, made the arrangements over the phone to have the icebox brought to the police station. The coroner would get the body to the morgue and try to figure out who the victim was and how she was murdered.

Deputy Turner walked in, hearing the end of the conversation. "What do you want me to do, Sheriff?"

He told him about the call and the body "Find out who might have had use for an old fashioned icebox. Maybe a school theater department or one of the hotels for a stage show. Even try a couple of those places that sell dry ice. See if we can find where it came from and then how it got to the desert with a woman's body in it."

This body had been found twenty-four hours after the Zimmermans arrived along with a dead body on their flight from Manhattan to Las Vegas.

Deputy Turner turned to the sheriff of Clark County. "Makes you wonder doesn't it?"

"Wonder what?"

"If the Zimmermans bring bad luck to our fair city?"

Sheriff Foster stood up, shaking his head. "Anything is possible with them. They give me a damn headache."

Foster found himself thinking about The Mob Museum in downtown Las Vegas. It had opened with a bang and declared "Whether you like it or not, this is American history." Indeed it was. A history of many years, many mobsters and many murders that took place in and around Las Vegas. Now he had another dead body on his hands. Muttering he said, "What the hell is this all about?"

"Sure, we used it years ago in a production of *I Remember Mama.*"

Turner was asking the head of the University

Theater Department about productions, where an ice-box would have been kept, and who could have access to it.

"It was kept in the prop storage room. We haven't used it for years. Almost anyone at the school could have gotten into that room, it's not usually locked."

"Could you ask around and see if anyone saw some people removing it?"

"Of course. What's this all about?"

"It was found out in the desert with a dead body inside."

Chapter Eleven

Krupe

Kris "Krupe" Carlson, a drummer for over thirty-five years, was nicknamed after his idol and drummer, Gene Krupa. Kris's hair was tied in a long grey ponytail, and he wore his usual outfit of jeans, a white button down shirt, and one of his collection of scarves that he'd found at a thrift store. He loved two things the most, music, especially jazz, and women.

"Sure, I enjoy the company of women." It was a simple statement, not meant to be anymore, not when being questioned by the sheriff's office.

"We heard from several people, including a couple friends of the dead woman, who said you had been seen together." Deputy Turner had seen Krupe banging away at his drums a number of times, at jazz clubs and bars around town

He was telling Turner what he knew about the woman stuffed in the icebox found in the desert. "Shannon Flynn was forty-six. A pretty Irish lady. I've known her for half a dozen years. She worked most recently at The Black Tie Casino. What happened?"

"She was found dead. When was the last time you saw her?"

"Shannon showed up last week at one of the clubs where I was playing, told me she was scared and leaving Vegas. Came to say goodbye to me."

"Did she say what kind of trouble?"

"No, but she seemed really scared. When I asked her if she wanted to talk, she told me it could be bad for me and she better not."

"Did she talk to anyone else there that night?"

"I don't think so. After talking to me, she left and it was the last I've seen of her. Please, can you tell me what happened? She was my friend."

"Krupe, Shannon Flynn was obviously murdered. Someone wanted to shut her up in a big way."

"Who?"

"We don't know. We're hoping you might have some idea. We could use your help."

"You don't think I did this, do you?"

"No. We've already checked with your work. There's no way you could have done this. Any thoughts on who could?"

"What about Rothstein at Black Tie?"

"Why would Benjamin Rothstein want to harm her?"

"Not Benjamin. His son Kody."

Krupe's lifestyle got him into trouble over the years. He never made much money. What he found humorous, others found crass or inappropriate, which sometimes would cost him work. A few times he found himself involved with someone else's wife. The police would eventually learn he and Jane Kohl were lovers.

For a short time.

Chapter Twelve

Poisoned Flask

Z achary Kohl always put a flask filled with bourbon in his brief case when he traveled by air, being a nervous traveler.

"Get it ready. I'm leaving shortly." A bully and a boor, he ordered the male housekeeper around without any pleasantries.

The housekeeper had his own agenda. He too had been sleeping with Jane Kohl for the past year. It was very rewarding, in more ways than one.

"For the right price," he told her. "Why not?"

By the time anyone figured out he had poisoned Zachary Kohl, he'd be out of the country somewhere where there was no extradition. His murder would be Mrs. Kohl's problem, and she would have proof she had flown to Las Vegas a couple days ahead of her husband's murder.

"Think your husband knows about us?"

"Maybe. I certainly don't care."

"Okay. Be sure people see you, know that you've been there a couple of days and could have had nothing to do with what happens to him."

"I intend to."

"Staying at The Black Tie?"

"Of course." Jane thought about how annoyed Benjamin would be to see her there. "Enjoy your new life, wherever it is. Best, I don't know."

"I will. Funny, isn't it, someone you once thought you loved…how those feelings can turn to hatred?"

"Yes, and dangerous," Jane said with a nod. "At least for my soon to be dead husband."

"Third time to Vegas this month, Mr. Kohl?"

"Yeah." Grabbing his flask, Kohl, took a huge swallow then threw it into his briefcase, thinking, "I'm never coming back. I know this jerk has been sleeping with the princess. I have a surprise for her, too, once I get to Vegas."

Inside the bus station locker number 438 would be what he required to follow through on the hired hit. It wouldn't be the first time he'd knocked someone off. Only this time it was much more personal and he was being paid a lot of money for the job. Plus, while he was in Vegas he figured he could collect some other monies owed to him.

"Hell of a deal." He was gloating on the way to catch the flight to Vegas.

He was at heart a revolting man with no morals, few, if any boundaries and even less self-awareness of how obnoxious he really was. He had told himself, "When I finish this job, I'll leave the country and start over somewhere like Brazil. The women there are hot."

Sitting on the plane fantasizing about beautiful women, he felt ill, figuring it was nerves from his fear of flying. After a while he leaned back and closed his eyes.

He never opened them again.

Kohl was a dead man flying.

Chapter Thirteen

The Black Tie

The Black Tie Hotel and Casino, a few blocks off the Vegas Strip, was not for families with little children putting their hands in a high-end dinner buffet. It was also not for people gambling with "scared money," money they could not afford to lose.

Each elegant room was a five-star deluxe suite in a hotel offering exceptional amenities designed for a sophisticated visitor. A private suite for whales, big money gamblers, was on a floor of its own. The main casino floor appeared like a black tie event where attractive young, shapely women offered free drinks wearing skimpy costumes of black shorts and a sleeveless vest with a black tie.

On the top floor were suites for long-term guests, those staying several months or more. Benjamin Rothstein, co-owner with his wife Deidre, kept a suite year-round for the many privileges it provided a man whose second marriage ended less than two years after it began. The first one lasted over twenty years, living together more like roommates than a marriage, and producing one son, a burden more than a pleasure.

Conversations with his son Kody were the same

over the last dozen years. "I need more money. I've been arrested for smoking pot. They found drugs in my car."

Benjamin Rothstein decided it was time Kody dealt with the consequences of his behavior. Giving little more thought to him, he allowed himself to gloat about The Black Tie. Zachary Kohl and he, it seemed, were two of a kind. Self deluded bullies, braggarts and full of themselves. In aging they were fat with bloated faces, thinning hair and were driven by greed that could barely be satisfied. Their enormous egos took care of that.

The hotel had a Five Star steak restaurant, a highly recommended buffet with gourmet offerings from lobster to lamb soaked in truffle sauce and desserts meant for decadence. It also had the best breakfast in town according to the official Vegas Visitors guide.

"When you're in Las Vegas, and haven't lost all your money, be sure to visit the Tuxedo Café in The Black Tie Hotel and Casino. It's worth the couple block walk from the Strip. Delicious food, especially breakfast which is served twenty-four hours a day, and The Temptation Coffee and Pastry Bar situated along one side of the Café is truly a temptation."

Locals and visitors came for the fairly affordable Tuxedo Café breakfast, some only to sit on one of the hot pink leather stools at the Temptation Bar for a choice of over twelve coffees and fresh baked croissants, muffins, scones or mini quiche. The counter was in black lacquer as were the backs of the stools facing a floor to ceiling mirror showing most of the café. Intentionally, there was an area off to one side reserved for those who wanted privacy.

"Is he here yet?"

"I don't see him. I left a message for Mr. Rothstein

you wanted to speak with him."

"I'll have another coffee."

"Anything to eat?"

"No thanks."

Jane Kohl was sitting in The Tuxedo Café as she had the past couple mornings. Asking for Benjamin Rothstein so waiters would be sure to remember her. She and he had known each other a long time, in business and in bed.

Jane chose her sexual partners based on what they had to offer her ranging from physical pleasures to money, connections and personal favors.

At one point the security manager came over. "Nice to see you again, Mrs. Kohl. I've been told to let you know he's not available, but suggest perhaps you could meet for drinks this evening."

"That's fine, Glenn. I'm also waiting for my husband to arrive from New York. Something seems to have delayed him."

Glenn Erickson, The Black Tie Security Manger protected Benjamin Rothstein and kept watch on happenings in the hotel and casino. Big money could bring big problems. He usually worked from six in the morning to six at night six days a week. The morning schedule was critical to most Vegas establishments since winners might be boisterous and celebrating, losers, whining and drinking way too much.

Glenn was short, stocky, with a full head of dark brown hair. In his mid-forties, he was tough in talk and build. On his days off Erickson went to a far less elegant coffee shop for his breakfast where he began to write some of the funny, bizarre happenings he would see. Telling his wife of over fifteen years, "Maybe I'll write a book about it someday."

He would read to her what he had seen, the two of them laughing as the television blasted the latest news disaster. They had no children, never wanted them and the money he made working for Benjamin Rothstein provided him a comfortable lifestyle in Vegas and car trips in the U.S. a couple times a year.

"Wait until you hear this one."

Glenn grabbed a cold beer from the refrigerator.

"This guy is there almost every day. Sits in the same place, sets up his computer. Not sure what he is doing, writing or maybe looking at porn. At any rate close to noon he goes out to his car and brings back a lunch bag. He takes out a hot dog roll and spreads it with mustard from a plastic jar he brought with him. Then, unbelievably, he unwraps a small roll of hard salami, cuts off about six slices and fixes himself a sandwich. I mean he's in a coffee shop. They sell sandwiches. Don't you think they should throw him out?"

"Maybe."

Raising his voice to make a point, he said, "They should throw him out."

Glenn's wife stood up and gave him a hug, "Of course, you're right."

"I'm telling you there's a book here with these crazy stories."

"Speaking of crazy stories, what's happening with your brother?"

"Haven't heard from Gordi for a few days. Last I saw him he was hanging out with Kody Rothstein."

"That can't be good."

"Nothing either of them does is good. They're both

trouble."

Chapter Fourteen

The Grieving Widow

"Yes, it's my husband, Zachary Kohl."

Having identified the body, the coroner pulled the sheet back over the dead man and the sheriff walked Jane back to his office to question her about her husband's death.

"He was murdered, ma'am."

"Don't be ridiculous. Who would want to murder him?"

"I assure you, I am not being the least bit ridiculous."

Shedding a few tears, adding in a bit of weeping, Jane glanced at the sheriff. "I have no idea who could do such a terrible thing. I've been in Vegas waiting for him. How was he murdered?"

"Poisoned. Do you have any idea who might have added arsenic to your husband's flask?"

Feigning shock, Jane Kohl, acting the grieving widow, said, "Not really."

"What does that mean?" Sheriff Foster did not like the questionable tone of her answer. "You sound unsure, like maybe you might know."

"Any time he travelled by plane his housekeeper made sure his flask was full and ready for him. He was scared to death to fly."

"Apparently he had reason to be."

"What does that mean?"

"Mrs. Kohl."

"Please, call me Jane."

Ignoring her, he said, "Mrs. Kohl, have you spoken to your housekeeper recently or before you left New York?"

"He was at the apartment talking to my husband, helping him pack. I left to catch my flight to Vegas."

"He's not there now. We have no idea where he is, certainly nowhere in New York."

The sheriff had a bad feeling about Jane Kohl, nothing he could be sure of, just a gut feeling that kept him tough and wise the past forty years. Her answers seemed rehearsed and tears coming and going almost on cue didn't sit well with him.

"Why are you in Vegas?"

"I have a business meeting with Benjamin Rothstein and a group of casino investors."

"I'm not sure how long you plan on staying but don't leave until I've said you can."

"Are you accusing me of something? Do I need an attorney?"

"No I'm not Mrs. Kohl. As for an attorney, that's up to you. Your husband was murdered on his way to Las Vegas, found dead on the plane. Someone killed him."

"I told you I was already here."

"Yes, you did."

With that final comment, Sheriff Foster stood up, called one of his officers to escort Mrs. Kohl from the station, and reminded her as he walked away, "Don't leave Vegas. We'll need to talk again, soon."

♦ ♣ ♥ ♠

Jane found it easy to cry. Early on she realized, with a few tears, her father let her get away with almost anything and everything, much to her mother's displeasure and disagreement.

He would tell her, wiping away her tears, "Sweetheart, I can't stand to see my little girl cry." He would hold her, hug her, telling her everything would be okay, while her mother told him, "She's going to be a handful when she grows up if you don't stop this nonsense."

By twelve she was a handful for sure, by sixteen out of control, and by eighteen, equipped with a brand new convertible from her father, she had the freedom to come and go as she pleased.

"Sweetheart, remember boys are interested in only one thing from a beautiful girl like you."

"Don't worry, Daddy, I promise to make you proud of me."

Luckily neither of Jane's parents lived to see her grow into a woman with few scruples and even less morals. Her mother warned her father over and over, "You better watch it. She's growing up to think she can get away with murder, thanks to you."

She was Daddy's Little Girl. He ignored such sage advice.

Chapter Fifteen

Cloud

"She has a bit of a temper."

"What does that mean?"

"It means she's sensitive."

Dora grilled Zero about his new friend. Dick was ignoring them.

"Zero, you're being vague about her."

"We met through an online gambling site then we started emailing each other and when I told her I was driving from Manhattan to Las Vegas she invited me to visit her. I did."

"Did you stay with her?"

"What are you, my mother?"

"You just met her and you're bringing her here? Not like you."

"Lady D," he said, using the name he'd called her since they were in high-school together, "enough. You'll meet her and I promise you, I'm not getting married."

"But—"

Click, again.

Zero hung up. He realized Dora wouldn't be happy until she knew more about Cloud.

"Dora wants to know all about you."

Laughing and agreeing about her temper, she said, "Tell her I was raised on an Indian pueblo outside of Grants, New Mexico, was awarded a scholarship to University of New Mexico in Albuquerque, then graduated with a degree in business. I was eight when my father died, old enough to miss him. My mother and two younger brothers still live on the pueblo. Once I left, I knew I would never live there again. I found the poverty and life style smothering. I don't visit often and I help them when I can. Think that should satisfy her for now?"

"Are you kidding? Dora will want to know what you eat for breakfast."

"Great. Tell her steak and eggs to keep me tough."

Smiling in a way that suggested a confidence between them, she said, "I do like to gamble some."

"Doesn't fit who you are," he told her as they ate dinner at one of the best Mexican restaurants he'd ever been to. Located in the heart of Albuquerque's Old Town, it faced a square where during the day Indian crafters sat outside and sold their pottery and jewelry.

Looking out the restaurant window they saw storm clouds gathering. "That could be a warning," Cloud told him.

"To us?"

"Perhaps. Too many people are doing bad things, denying others their rights, taking away their dignity for greed and power."

Cloud looked at Zero when he asked her, "Does that frighten you?"

"No. I see them as a warning to be cautious."

"About me?"

Bursting out in laughter, Cloud reached over the table and kissed Zero, and not on the cheek. Their getting to know each other conversation went on well past midnight. A city with little nightlife and few places open late, the streets were nearly silent when they left.

Cloud went home to her apartment on the west side, across the dry and muddy Rio Grande River, where one can see the lights of the city and the sunsets over the Sandia Mountains.

Zero went to his hotel in the center of the city, across from a shopping center, movie theater and restaurants. He was philosophical about the people he saw when he took these road trips. Seeing faces in a country filled with so many differences he wondered about their lives and whether anyone's was really much different from his.

At noon the next day, they met at the Frontier Restaurant, across from the University of New Mexico, known for the best cinnamon buns and red or green chili on anything and everything. After another two hours, Zero stood up to pay the check in a restaurant filled with mostly students and a few homeless people, when he blurted out the invitation, "Cloud, come with me to Vegas."

She didn't skip a beat. "As long as I can ride there with you."

It was as simple as that, and in time, would become as complicated, thanks to unforeseen events and unexpected feelings.

At seven the following morning, Zero the Bookie and Cloud, who gave him no last name, were on the road together with endless conversation.

"For your information, I pay my own way."

"You mean I can't bribe you with my charm?"

"From what I heard of your phone conversation

with someone called Lady D your charm is wanting."

"You'll meet her and her husband in Vegas."

"Spend much time with them?"

"Yes. They seem to get involved in murders and for some reason I seem to get caught up in it with them."

Startled, Cloud put her hand on Zero's knee. "They murder people?"

Taking her hand, gently touching it, "No solving them."

"Oh. I was ready to pull out my gun."

Taking his hand away, keeping his eyes on the road he asked, "You carry a gun?"

"Lady alone needs protection."

"Not from me."

"Good to know. What about your friends?"

"No gun needed with them. They're retired. He was a lawyer. She was a judge. Although…"

"Although what?" Cloud's voice raised in concern.

"She did find a dead body on their plane to Las Vegas."

Cloud turned to gaze out the window at the passing desert landscape. Reaching into her bag to feel her gun, she wondered, "What have I gotten myself into?"

Chapter Sixteen

Hating Each Other

Benjamin and Deidre Rothstein's marriage began out of deceit by cheating on their spouses, and after the lust wore off they were faced with each other's ugly truths complicated by secrets, and the fact neither of them were nice people. Quite the opposite.

Before marriage they had become business partners in The Black Tie Hotel and Casino. She had money to invest. Benjamin so loved money and anyone who had it. But for a time, business turned to pleasure, only to continue to a marriage and one where ultimately hatred was the prime emotion. She had admired his business abilities. He had admired her body and interest in sharing it with him once in a while.

Benjamin, who behaved bizarrely at times, had not grown old gracefully. His love of excess with alcohol, food, especially sweets, helped the sixty-four year old man grow fat. At a little under five-foot-seven, he was not a pretty sight. His money kept other women interested. A few thought they might become the next Mrs. Rothstein.

"No more marriages for me. I can get all the broads I want," he said. Dick had known him for years but they were never close friends.

"He's too cunning and insincere for my taste," Dick had told Dora.

Deidre was cunning and manipulative in her own quiet way. She had her own money, her own bank accounts and her own investments. Their marriage was filled with secrets, affairs, hate and worse.

Fifteen years younger than Benjamin, she was a good-looking woman who stayed youthful and slim. Deidre lived in Vegas all her life. Her Mormon father came from Utah after his wife died and bought land eventually worth a great deal of money. Money he left his only daughter and two sons. He nurtured her, "my smart little girl," knowing she was not only smarter but tougher than her older brothers.

"Deidre, you have to know who you can trust, who wants something from you, and how to negotiate for what you want. There's a world of hate and jealousy out there. You'll be a very rich woman. Keep the money in the family."

When her father was ill, near death, she asked him softly, "Do you want me to continue with the family business."

His one word response: "Yes."

She would do that and do it very well. It also meant she had no plans to have children. Her brothers were enough of a responsibility and burden.

Benjamin's one son from his first marriage, Kody, was often in trouble with the law and constantly in need of money. At forty, he was pretty much beyond being anything more than his father's flunky, motivated by money. Money he needed for drinking and drugs. Once a good looking young man, the years had turned him skinny, with all sorts of twitches from his bad habits. Kody knew Zachary Kohl.

He also knew the person found dead in the desert. "Poor Kody," the Black Tie Security Manager, Glenn Erickson told his wife. "His father bullies and humiliates him and controls him with women and money. He's grown up arrogant, vulnerable and unable to get out of his own way. Been arrested a number of times."

Dick and Dora knew not to mention him to Benjamin. "Do you think he's the cause of his son's problems?" Dora had asked. She had been enjoying a gourmet coffee at The Tuxedo Café when they saw Kody yelling at a young woman who worked at The Black Tie Casino.

Dick couldn't help himself, he got up and walked over to Kody who looked like he was about to slap her. "Hey Kody, Dora and I were hoping you would join us for breakfast."

Letting go of her, without saying a word, he turned and stormed out of the café. The girl looked terrified, nodded a thank you and ran the other way in tears. Kody Rothstein's behavior was going to take him down a dangerous rabbit hole. Unfortunately others would suffer the fall with him.

Kody had learned to hate his father when he was a young boy. His father's cruel remarks knew no boundaries. The problem was he also needed him, or at least his money, until someone else came along with a better offer.

Which it did. Sealing his fate and not a pleasant one.

Chapter Seventeen

Falling

"How did you know him?" The sheriff was in the interrogation room with Kody Rothstein.

"He was a high roller in one of our casinos."

"Were you friends?"

"No, Sheriff, and why are you bothering me? Where is my lawyer? My father said he would be here."

Kody was sweating, legs crossing and uncrossing, his face showed several days growth of a beard, making it look more like a dark shadow on his face. Glancing up at the clock ticking minutes away, Kody felt like the room was getting smaller and darker. This was how his panic attacks started.

"According to your phone records you spoke to Zachary Kohl over two dozen times in the past month. Why?"

"I was trying to collect money he owed the casino and me. I wanted to know when he would be here to settle up."

"Did you know he was on his way here?"

"Yeah, he emailed me a few days ago, said he had our money."

"Why are you so nervous?" the sheriff asked.

"My father will be furious I did business with him."

"Kody, I think you're lying. You owed him money, didn't you?"

Sheriff Foster knew Kody Rothstein was on drugs and ready to explode.

"Yeah, so what? It's none of your business."

Now in a cold sweat, breathing heavy, Kody was close to experiencing a full blown panic attack.

"How much money did you owe him?"

His mouth twitching, trying to gain his composure, Kody didn't respond.

"Kody, how much money did you owe Zachary Kohl?" Sheriff Foster was shouting at him.

Screaming and holding his head, he replied, "I don't feel well. I need to get out of here."

Standing over him, leaning close into Kody's face the sheriff asked him, "Again Kody. How much did you owe Kohl?"

"Almost a million dollars."

"He threatened to tell your father. Right?"

"YES!" With that Kody passed out and fell off the chair.

"What are you doing here?"

Kody glanced up at his father from the hospital room where he had been taken after passing out. Benjamin Rothstein stood next to his son's bed, shaking his head.

"Waiting for you to tell me what's going on?"

"I had one of my panic attacks and I guess I passed out. Don't remember anything," Kody lied.

"Why were you at the police station?" Benjamin

said, obviously annoyed.

"The police were asking about some dead guy. They say he was murdered."

"Did you know him?"

"Sure, he used to play at our casinos." Kody did not meet his father's glare.

"You're lying," said Benjamin.

"I'm sick, go away."

"You're sick alright. You're a junkie and a compulsive liar. The sheriff told me about you owing Kohl money. You can consider your stay here the last of anything the company, or I pay for. I'm done with you." Benjamin was seething.

"You'll be sorry," Kody shouted to his father's back.

Benjamin Rothstein also knew Zachary Kohl all too well. He had his own relationship with the man as well as the man's wife.

Telling himself as he left the hospital, "That stupid kid is going to cause me big problems."

That was an understatement. The rabbit hole had plenty of room.

Chapter Eighteen

Black Tie Steak House

Zero and Cloud arrived early afternoon, unpacked, rested and dressed for dinner with Dick and Dora.

"You can stay with me. Plenty of room." Zero had one of the smaller two-bedroom condos at The Star, three floors below the Zimmermans.

"Best not. I already made reservations at The Black Tie Hotel. It seemed convenient. "Cloud had other motives. It was important she stay there.

"I'll meet you at seven at the restaurant. I'll be the hot chick in a red dress," she told him.

And she was. Dora took one look at her and raised her eyebrows at the attractive woman who seemed to have captured Zero's heart, or at least his interest. Cloud watching, didn't say anything. Out of a sense of caution, she touched her purse.

The restaurant tables were set with expensive linens, china and white orchids. It was busy with influential people, most with a sense of self-importance too often dictating their behaviors and attitudes. Benjamin was sitting with a group who were raising their voices in what didn't seem too friendly a conversation.

Dora reaching over to Dick said softly, "Who are

those people with Rothstein?"

"Never saw them. Zero, you know them?"

Zero shook his head while Dora curiously eyed Cloud who glanced over at the table several times, like she knew someone or something.

After Rothstein's dinner companions left he stopped over to say hello to the Zimmermans and Zero, both had known him and his not so great reputation for many years.

"Welcome back. Who do we have here?" he said, nodding at Cloud. Zero stood up, put his arm around Rothstein and whispered, "Behave," and introduced her. Rothstein said, "You're lovely my dear." Cloud stared up at him, gave a slight smile and didn't say a word.

More and more, Dora wondered what her story was. "Cloud, join me for lunch one day. I've been dying to try a new place that just opened in Henderson."

Cloud smiled, "Let me know. I'm staying here at The Black Tie." Cloud knew Dora wanted to check her out. She thought that maybe Dora could be helpful to her too.

Gourmet meals and drinks covered the dining room tables and conversations both loud and whispered were taking place throughout the restaurant. Rothstein, still standing by the table, pushed Zero's arm away and called, almost shouted, to a waiter, "Bring more drinks here. On the house."

Suddenly a man dressed head to toe in black appeared. His face covered, he shot twice at Benjamin Rothstein. On instinct Dick pushed Dora and Cloud to the floor as the man dressed like a ninja ran out a side door.

"Benjamin, are you hit?" Dick looked up and saw him standing there grinning.

"Nah missed me by a mile."

"Have you been getting death threats?" Dick asked

"Hey, casino owners are targets for losers."

Security on duty had acted quickly, calling the police and checking where the gunman had exited and conveniently escaped. One of them texted what happened to Glenn Erickson.

The restaurant emptied out quickly and there were now shadows on the walls from waiters and bus boys moving through the restaurant as if in slow motion. Fear registered on their faces.

Benjamin was acting surprisingly calm. His demeanor bothered Dora more than anything. She leaned over to Dick and said, "This is very odd."

Dick, never a fool, thought so too.

One of the waiters showed the sheriff the scene. "The gunman fled out this side door. Seems as if he or she knew their way around here."

Checking outside, Sheriff Foster saw a narrow passageway behind the hotel. He could see flashing lights flickering out front as a couple of his officers walked to the area where the shooter had disappeared into the crowded city streets.

Deputy Turner asked each of the staff on duty, "Any idea who it was?"

No one had a clue.

At least not anyone who would admit it.

The Zimmermans, Zero and Cloud were also questioned about what they had witnessed. "Why am I not surprised you're here. Turner, get their statements and let them leave."

"Sheriff, we…"

"I know, Dick, you just happened to be having dinner here."

"Well, yes."

"I hope you're going back to New York soon."

Dora put her arm around Dick. "And miss all this fun?"

Chapter Nineteen

Plain Jane

With what amounted to a hit out on her man, Jane Kohl was clearly not singing or even humming "Stand by Your Man."

Waiting in the lobby of The Black Tie Hotel, dressed in a tight, sleeveless black dress, black net stockings, three inch heels, her new hairdo streaked with shades of blond, no one would call her Plain Jane this night.

Leaving the restaurant after what others considered a harrowing experience, a far less concerned Rothstein noticed the sexy lady giving him a look stopping him dead in his tracks.

Until she said his name.

"Hello, Benjamin. Don't you recognize me? I believe you've been avoiding me."

Startled, surprised and leering, he said, "You look fantastic."

Coming up to him, planting a kiss on his fat cheek, she replied, "See what you've been missing?"

"I've been busy the past few days. How about a drink now?"

"You mean busy with *our* Casino Syndicate? And

you didn't invite me? Benjy, what's a girl to do with you?"

Rothstein took her arm as if to lead her upstairs to his suite. Jane was having none of his B.S. She knew this man. They had been having sex together, off and on, for years. When in the same city at the same time, bored, restless, wanting uncomplicated passion, they took care of each other's physical desires.

Their relationship changed over the past year when she had been told by one of the others in the syndicate he was requesting meetings without her. His explanation to Jane was that a bunch of guys wanted to get together for drinks, no dames, and nothing else.

Jane had been kept informed about whatever nonsense he might be up to, especially in relation to her, and for a time she waited to see how far he would go in excluding her.

"Benjy, we have some catching up to do. I brought a couple more photos of you. Really lovely."

As they walked to The Black Tie Bar & Lounge, Dick and Dora caught sight of Rothstein whispering in her ear and putting his hand on her shapely behind.

"Charming, isn't he?" Dora put her arm through Dick's, and Zero and Cloud walked behind them.

"Not an hour after being shot at, the police are still here and he's playing around with some hot looking broad." Zero smiled.

Cloud reached out to Dora, surprising her. "Let's not wait. How about lunch tomorrow?"

Nodding yes and curious at the sudden decision, she said, "Sure. Buzz and I will pick you up here at twelve thirty."

Zero and Cloud said goodnight, while Dora suggested a drink to Dick.

"Who are you kidding, sweetheart? You want to see what Rothstein is up to."

"Me? I'm thirsty after all that excitement is all." Dora pretended shock at his comment.

"No, you're not."

"Fine. I still want a drink."

Rothstein saw them walk in, grinned and turned back to Jane. Sitting at one of the corner tables, half a dozen televisions blasting, some with sports and a couple with news, Jane literally kicked him under the table.

"Benjamin, I assume you know Zachary is dead."

"I heard he was murdered."

"Yes, so I've been told."

"Did you do it?"

"I was here in town when it happened. You should know, I've been trying to reach you."

"Okay. Did you arrange for someone else to do it?"

"Benjamin, I'm not so clever." Jane shrugged her shoulders.

"Oh, yes you are, my dear. What do you want from me?"

"Dear departed Zachary told me your son owed him money. Of course, some of your syndicate shares could pay his debt off nicely. Also it's time to cut the bull you've been trying to give me about the syndicate meetings. I know what you're up to and you're not going to get away with it. Remember, I do have those lovely photos of you."

Benjamin Rothstein, getting up to leave, leaned over to whisper in her ear, "Go to hell, bitch."

It was well past midnight, and every seat in the lounge was occupied. Dora was able to see Benjamin and his lady friend in the huge mirror behind the bar. She had not recognized Jane looking all hot and sexy. After he whispered in her ear she reached over, slapped him and asked the bartender for another drink.

Rothstein walked over to the Zimms, apologizing. "That lady is crazy, wanted me to pay her for sex. I get all the free tail I want."

Without another word, he patted Dick on the back, said goodnight and went toward the casino, making a call on his way there.

"Glenn, I know you're here. Come up to my suite. It's urgent."

Rothstein was not concerned about the gunshots. Jane Kohl was a much bigger problem, her and those photos.

"She's blackmailing me. She wants a bigger share of the casino syndicate so she's asking me to pay her off with more shares of it. We need to get this handled. Think your brother could help?" Benjamin was feigning concern, pacing like a caged lion. He stopped, looked at Glenn, then went back to pacing.

"You know him. He might make a bigger mess of things."

Glenn didn't believe or trust his boss and he could tell something was different with him, almost as if he was frightened.

Now he was anxious to make a call. "Never mind, I have an idea. I'll take care of it. You go see everything is settled downstairs with the police."

Glenn was sure things were going to become a bigger mess. Benjamin didn't want a problem taken care of, he wanted revenge.

He would know he was right if he'd heard Rothstein's call as he left his suite. "Kody, forget what I said at the hospital. If you want to make a lot of money, get over here. Ten o'clock tomorrow morning."

Chapter Twenty

Being Cautious

"Zero, how could she be so calm tonight?"

He had walked Cloud to her room, then went back to the bar to have a goodnight drink with Dick and Dora.

"She grew up on a reservation, poor and struggling to survive. I guess you learn how to handle difficult situations. At least she did."

"Still…"

"Both of you stop. I like her. I like her a lot, in fact. I don't know if we'll be anything more than friends but for now we make each other happy."

"I know. I'm sorry. You're family and…"

"We've been best friends since high school, Dora, but I haven't felt this way in a long time and you need to trust me. I'm not going to do anything foolish. I'm not getting married. I'm not giving her money. I'm not running off to live with her."

"We do trust you." Dora stood up and gave Zero a hug.

"Yeah, and you don't trust her. I get that."

"Well at least she didn't make fun of your yellow and green polka dot bow tie and orange shirt."

"Hey, they give me character."

"You are a character and we love you."

"Don't you think the whole gun shooting ninja was bizarre?" Zero sat back, directing the question to both Dick and Dora.

Dick nodded yes. "Maybe more to it."

"Like what?"

"No idea. And Dora is delighted to stay out of it too, aren't you?"

"Who me? I'm ready to say goodnight to you two."

"Everything okay?" he asked Cloud

"Yes. Maybe."

"Does he know?"

"Not yet. I have to tell him. He's a good man."

"You like him, don't you?"

"I do."

"Cloud, what we're doing is important."

"I know."

"If he's the good man you say he is, he'll understand."

Chapter Twenty-One

Why?

As the saying goes, "There's no such thing as a free lunch."

Cloud was waiting in front of her hotel, wearing light grey linen slacks and a darker grey top. Dora thought she looked stunning.

Buzz opened the door, was introduced to Zero's lady friend, and everyone smiled. He then drove them to lunch. Dora was wearing white slacks and a deep blue cotton sweater. Two women, out for lunch...actually much more.

Each had an agenda. Seated in a corner by a window, at their request, wanting privacy, drinks ordered, lunch menu on the table, the gloves were about to come off.

"Dora, I'm not married. I'm not a thief. I'm not out to hurt, scam, con or break Zero's heart. We fell in instant *like* with each other. We have no idea where this will go. Hard to know at our age."

Dora sat back, listening. Due to her years as a judge, she knew the importance of not having an immediate reply.

"Zero told you where I grew up and why I left. What

else do you want to know about me?" Cloud was almost challenging Dora with a slight grin, hands folded on the table in front of her.

"Why did you come to Las Vegas?"

"I wanted to enjoy some time with Zero, maybe gamble a little."

"And?"

"And what?"

"You're not a frivolous woman who's only out for some fun. I have the ability to read people, being a judge for as many years as I was."

Cloud sat back and met Dora's gaze. They had waved the waiter away twice already.

"You think I plan on doing something bad to Zero?"

"I don't know. Do you?"

"Good grief. No."

"Then what?"

"Let's order."

"Can you honestly tell me you have no other purpose for coming to Las Vegas?"

"Does it matter?"

"Yes, Zero is family to us."

"Do you always distrust people who Zero spends time with?"

"Not usually."

"Why me?"

"He likes you."

"I like him."

"Why were you looking to meet someone on an online gambling site?"

"Same as Zero. To make new friends with similar interests."

The waiter came over to announce the lunch specials. The restaurant was now crowded. People were waiting for seats.

Both women ordered the lunch special and a glass of wine, then handed the menus back to the good looking waiter who obviously wanted them fed and out. Turn-over meant more tips.

As he walked away, Dora leaned forward, elbows on the table, hands crossed, and stared at Cloud.

"You're not going to let this go, are you?" Cloud asked.

Dora shook her head slightly.

Cloud sat quiet, thinking.

"Not a chance," Dora finally said. "Dick says I'm like a puppy with a new chew toy. You can't get anything away from me." Dora leaned closer over the table toward Cloud. "Tell me. What gives?"

Cloud reached into her leather shoulder bag, took out a card and handed it to Dora.

"Can you tell me any more?" Dora asked.

"Not now. And Zero can't know for now. I will tell him when the time is right," Cloud said.

"Why?"

"It's better that way."

"Fine then. Under these circumstances, lunch is on you." Dora said with a smile of relief.

Chapter Twenty-Two

Casino Syndicate

R eservation shopping. The casino syndicate was in a position to set up a new spot on an Indian reservation. While legal, few deals were ever completed due to complications.

Benjamin Rothstein and Jane Kohl were part of a syndicate previously accused of attempting to defraud Native tribes who owned casinos. So far they had cleverly hidden behind laws and lawyers. So far.

"Benjamin, we've been working on this project for over six years, now you're telling us you want more money for payoffs to get that casino built?"

Sitting at a large round table in a far corner of The Black Tie Dining Room, questions were being asked, causing Benjamin plenty of concern. It was a contentious meeting and he was in the hot seat.

"How much have you taken for your own gain?"

"Nothing. Check the books."

"We are, and why isn't Jane Kohl at this meeting?"

"I don't know."

"We know you never told her about it. Does she have something on you?"

"Bull, her husband was murdered. Guess she's

grieving."

"Not Jane."

"I don't give a damn about her at the moment."

His face was red and swollen from anger. His body language looked like he wanted to choke someone, his words full of fury as Deidre's words screamed in his head.

"Your desperation is showing. Your lying, cheating and scheming are catching up with you. It's causing you to act careless, Benjamin. They'll take you down and I certainly don't intend to do anything to stop them."

"We took a vote before coming here. You're off the project. One of us will be taking over."

"Hell you are."

"You can no longer access casino syndicate funds."

"I'll take you to court."

Breaking out in laughter, the spokesperson for the group told him, "Go ahead. I expect it should make a good story. The owner of The Black Tie Hotel and Casino accused of embezzling funds earmarked for a Native tribal casino. We requested we meet in public so there would be an audience witnessing this get together and preventing you from ranting too much."

This was what the shouting had been all about at dinner. It was why Cloud was watching it without completely staring the whole time. She had a close relationship with one of the members of the syndicate. They pretended not to know each other.

The impact on Native Americans as a result of tribal gaming offered both positive finances and negative consequences. Fortunately the Indian Gaming Working Group was formed to help address many of the criminal acts related to Native gaming.

Rothstein didn't give a damn about any of it. He was caught with his hand in the cookie jar and was about to get it smashed good.

For Benjamin, when things didn't go his way, his thoughts turned to vicious acts and he was about to be totally out of control in what he planned to do next.

Chapter Twenty-Three

Dora's Dilemma

S he knew what was coming.

"How was lunch with Cloud? I assume you've information to share."

There it was.

Dora and Dick believed the strength of their long marriage, in addition to loving each other, was honesty and a willingness to communicate, even when they were upset or concerned about something.

Of course, there were a few times Dora got involved with criminals and murderers when Dick didn't want her to, or engaged in sneaky actions like keeping Zachary Kohl's key. This was different. Dora had made a promise to Cloud.

They were meeting Zero and Cloud in The Tuxedo Café for a casual dinner around eight. They had time for a drink at home first as they watched the insanity known as the news.

"Why aren't you answering me?"

Dick turned off the television suspecting there was more to her silence.

"What gives?"

Their spacious Las Vegas condo, The Star was decorated in desert colors of tan, beige and cream tones with beautiful pillows, lamps and pottery in shades of orange and turquoise. Every room carried through the same colors in different tones and there were pictures on the wall by famous Southwestern and Indian artists. Turning on a beautiful lamp with a turquoise base and cream color shade, the evening light fading, Dora sat down next to Dick.

"Dora, you're up to something."

"Who me?"

"Yes, dear. You."

"I promised Cloud not to tell anyone."

"Tell anyone what?"

"Well, sweetheart, if I tell you what, then I've told you."

"You're talking in circles."

"Oh good. Then you can ignore me and we can dress for dinner."

"I'm dressed. We're only going to the café."

"True. Still, I need to change." She walked into the bedroom, Dick followed her, knowing how easily his wife could get herself into trouble.

Watching her slip off her robe, he thought how remarkable and lovely she was, even after all these years.

"Dora, you need to tell me what's going on."

"You're adorable when you're clever. No, I can't."

"You're not adorable at all at the moment."

"Dick, really, this is a bit of a dilemma for me. I don't want to be secretive, I can't betray her trust."

"What about Zero and my trust?"

"See, there's the dilemma."

"No. I don't see."

"Sure you do. You're just annoyed I won't tell you."

"Of course I am. I'm also concerned what you might be up to now."

"Me?" Dora dripped with humorous sarcasm.

"Okay, don't tell me."

"See how easy that was for you to agree with me?" Dora grinned.

Dick walked back to the living room and downed the rest of his drink, mumbling, "Dora and Cloud, this is only going to lead to trouble."

Chapter Twenty-Four

More Questions than Answers

Solving the murders of Zachary Kohl and the woman in the icebox was progressing much too slowly for Sheriff Foster. Jane Kohl and Benjamin Rothstein had been brought in for questioning again. He wanted to see how they acted when they were in the interrogation room together. Foster realized that if looks could kill, these two would both be dead.

"Why are we here?" Rothstein said, visibly annoyed.

"Her husband has been murdered. Phone records prove you've spoken to each other often."

"We have business together," volunteered an equally annoyed Jane.

"Might be you wanted to get rid of him so you two could be together."

"You must be kidding. We don't even like each other. Sheriff, I believe Benjamin is concerned about problems he's having with our business partners. As for our previous private life together, that was off and on and very off now. Look at him, little fat man."

Jane sat there gloating as Rothstein was nearly frothing at the mouth, "She's hardly my type. I like them young and hot."

"Both of you shut up," shouted Sheriff Foster. Glaring at Jane, he asked her, "Did you murder your husband?"

"I told you last time, no, no, no."

"What about you, Rothstein?" Foster slammed his fist on the table.

"How the hell could I have accomplished that feat? I live here."

"Either one or both of you could have arranged the murder."

"Well, I didn't, and if you have any more questions, talk to my attorney."

"Something we agree on." Jane stood up, grabbed her purse and slammed the door on the way out.

Rothstein practically knocked over the chair as he left.

"Housekeeper's gone," the Manhattan detective told Sheriff Foster. "Seems he left after Kohl did, then went to the airport and took a flight out of the country."

"Okay. Let's keep each other updated with any new information."

Both agreed.

There was nothing, so far, to link Jane Kohl to her husband's murder. The investigation proved the house-keeper bought the arsenic, and most likely added it to the flask. Only his and the victim's fingerprints were on the outside of it and on the screw on cap.

Jane could easily prove she was in Las Vegas at the time.

"Damn convenient if you ask me." After forty years

in law enforcement, the sheriff trusted his gut. Right now it was telling him these two characters were involved and more trouble from them was on the way.

How right he was.

Chapter Twenty-Five

Brothers for Hire

"Gordi, meet me at the bar outside of town. I need to talk to you about Benjamin Rothstein."

They were sitting across from each other in a small booth at The Underworld Saloon. It was quiet except for a few hardcore drinkers. Dark as always, it was a good place to discuss secret plans. Where a slight nod of the head meant the guy across from you would do a favor you asked. It was where Glenn would meet his brother when they wanted to go unnoticed, where no one would give a damn about them. Or so they thought.

Benjamin didn't go there, of course. After he called Kody offering him a lot of money, he phoned Gordi Erickson. "I got a job I need you and Kody to do."

He called Glenn, "I decided to hire your brother to take care of something for me. Be sure he stays sober." Click.

Now, sitting across from Gordi, Glenn said, "Listen, I don't mind keeping some of Rothstein's secrets, but I don't want either of us to be party to murder." Glenn knew his boss was not a good man, but it was a heck of a good job.

"Maybe it's too late for that."

"What do you know?" Glenn reached over and pulled at his brother's dirty denim jacket. "What have you heard?"

"I'm not sure. Kody told me his father is acting crazy. He heard him call Deidre and say he needed money. Said his father is a dangerous guy who has done a lot of bad things."

"Yeah, I've covered for him many times, but never for murder. When he first hired me years ago it was with the agreement that what he did was kept private, in house. I've been fine with it, only this time seems different."

Gordi was downing his second beer, and calling for a third.

"Damn it, slow down or you're going to be drunk soon. I promised him I would be sure you stayed sober. What did he ask you to do when you met with him?"

Gordi already more than a little tipsy didn't give a damn about secrets or promises.

"Told us to threaten Jane Kohl. In fact he said to scare her to death if necessary."

"Why?"

"Says she's trying to blackmail him."

"Did he tell you why?"

"Glenn, you must be kidding, brother. He ain't going to tell me."

"Do you know who took a shot at him in the restaurant?"

Gordi was suddenly quiet.

"You do, don't you?"

"The man in black?" Gordi looked at his brother with a huge, goofy grin.

"Don't tell me that was you?"

"Kody hired me to scare his father."

"Why?"

"His father paid him and me each a thousand bucks to do it."

Glenn stood up, and slapped his brother across the face. Walking out, he turned and looked at him, sad for what he had become. "You idiot, that man will tell the sheriff it was you if he needs to in order to protect himself."

Gordi knew his brother was right. "So what," he said. "I'm going to figure out a way to get away from here."

Wishful thinking from someone already lost.

Chapter Twenty-Six

Gordi

Over six feet tall, with a beer belly, half dozen teeth missing and a gambling habit, Gordi was Glenn Erickson's younger brother by four years and looked twenty years older. He was a hard drinking hoodlum and a small time hustler in a big time town already devouring him.

A few hours after meeting Gordi at the bar, the sheriff's office called Glenn.

"Your brother is under arrest. He was drunk and carrying an unregistered gun. He was threatening someone, she said she feared for her life."

"I'll be right there."

It had rained for a few hours. Some streets were flooded and the early night sky was eerie with grayish clouds hovering in odd shapes.

The Native Americans who once inhabited this land would say it was an omen.

Gordi was in a cell, cursing. He fell over when he tried to stand up. "Drunk and disorderly but the lady is not pressing charges," the officer told Glenn. "We'll keep him overnight."

"Fine, I'll bail him out in the morning. Can I talk to

him for a minute?"

As the police officer walked away, Glenn once again grabbed Gordi. "You idiot, there's no way I can protect you from the police or Rothstein."

With that Gordi sat in his cell sobbing.

Chapter Twenty-Seven

Money from Deidre

Deidre broke out in laughter at what she thought was a clever remark. In recent years, Benjamin Rothstein only showed up when he needed money.

"You owe me."

"Hardly."

"Okay fine, then will you loan me the money?"

"What will I get in return?"

"Me. Alive."

"Oh please. I don't give a damn about you."

"What the hell kind of wife are you?"

"One who's thought little of you for years except as a business associate."

"What will you do if they kill me?"

"Hang your head on the wall like a dead deer, my dear!" That's what made her laugh. "Oh, and I'll get to own all of The Black Tie."

Deidre's home on two acres of desert land, outside of Summerlin, Nevada was a wise investment, complete with a few horses. The affluent area, with beautiful homes, views and access to the night life of Las Vegas had been listed as one of the "Best Places to Live in America," according to *Money* magazine. Too bad Benjamin hadn't paid attention. His lifestyle and behavior were costing him dearly.

They were sitting in her den with huge windows facing away from the city, small bottles of sparkling water on a table. "You've lost money gambling, on bad investments, scamming and scheming and bedding all sorts of women. Why should I help you?"

Looking at the water bottles, he said, "What's this junk. I need a real drink."

"Then go to a bar. You're not getting drunk here."

"Deidre, I'm begging you. Okay, is that what you want? The truth is, someone is blackmailing me."

"Will they stop if you pay them?"

"I sure as hell hope so, or else."

"Or else what?" Deidre curled her slim legs up on the beautiful white leather sofa while Benjamin was pacing like a caged animal.

"Nothing, nothing at all."

"Is it a woman?"

"Yeah."

"Benjamin, dear, does she have photos of you?"

"Damn it, yes."

"See, I never cared. But I warned you someone would take advantage of your proclivities." Deidre grinned.

"You cared. And you think knowing gives you some kind of power over me." Benjamin was sweating, watching Deidre, thinking he would like another shot at her taut body.

"Oh darling, I have more than those photos to keep you running scared. There are two sets of books for The Black Tie and the syndicate...surely you wouldn't want anyone to know about those." Deidre stood up, glaring at

Benjamin. "Now it's time for you to get out of here."

Benjamin grabbed his jacket and walked out to his car, knowing he had to get rid of Jane, one way or another. Kody and Gordi had threatened Jane, but she wasn't scared. They took the money he'd given them and gotten high and drunk. Zachary Kohl died before he could make the hit he'd been hired to do.

"I'll probably have to do this myself. As for Deidre, the hell with her."

The only one who heard him was his ego, who believed Benjamin Rothstein could do whatever he wanted and get away with it.

Chapter Twenty-Eight

Eliminating a Problem

"**G**et my son to my suite."

Rothstein left Deidre's determined to eliminate his problem with Jane Kohl and deal with the casino syndicate.

Glenn was sitting at the coffee bar in the café when Rothstein came in all disheveled, face red and grabbing Glenn who had been waiting there for him.

"Where is my son?"

"Mr. Rothstein, I have no idea. I've left phone and email messages since you called me less than an hour ago. No answer."

"What?"

"I've also called places he hangs out. He's not at any of them."

"What about his mother?"

"Benjamin, they haven't spoken or seen each other in years."

"Did you ask your brother?"

"I made his bail earlier and he left ranting and raving about you causing him too much trouble and never wanting anything to do with you again."

"I don't give a damn. He messed up bigtime," Benjamin shouted.

"Well he didn't tell the sheriff's office it was you who hired him."

"Good for him. Now find Kody." He yelled even louder as he pushed Glenn.

"You shouldn't have done that, Boss." Glenn walked away, leaving Rothstein staring after him.

The two couples having a casual dinner at The Tuxedo Café were watching the scene play out. Dick being a smart aleck, commented, "Trouble in paradise."

"Darling, maybe a lover's fight?"

"Think I'll check on the big man." Dick walked over to Benjamin. "Anything we can do to help?"

"Huh? No. Thanks. Just a family problem."

With that Benjamin stormed out of the café, knocking over food and drink on a customer's table and going after Glenn. "Find him or find a new job."

Glenn knew, then and there, Benjamin Rothstein was in bigger trouble than he realized. He had to make a decision on what he was going to do next, or not.

Dick sat back down with Dora, Cloud and Zero. A waiter brought them their drink order. Everyone was stunned into silence, for the moment.

With a second round of drinks the conversation exploded, everyone talking all at once until Zero said, "Be quiet, we have an idea."

Dora looked questioningly across at Cloud, knowing what Cloud was really doing in Las Vegas, and not believing they would be getting married or doing any other such impulsive thing.

Dick quickly downed his second drink, sat back in his seat, arm around Dora and said, "Do tell."

"What do you mean, do tell?" Zero smiled, Cloud

acted coy. Seriously, only acting.

"Cut it out. You two have been acting like a couple of doting parents. Get over it and listen to us."

"Fine, what's the idea?"

"How to catch the murderers. Oh for god's sake, what did you think?"

"Zero, I believe they thought we were making a personal announcement."

"So what if we were?" Zero reached over and hugged Cloud who in turn gave him a long kiss.

"Seems we're two unseemly adults. What in the world are they to do with us?" Zero was laughing so hard the others were hushing him, only making him laugh more.

Dick intended to ask his wife later about her reaching over to Cloud, taking her hand in a way one might do with a close and caring friend.

The café had quieted down after Rothstein stormed out.

"Don't keep us waiting. You have a plan, tell us."

The waiter came to their table announced the evening specials as if he was on stage performing a soliloquy. Dinner was ordered and a decision made to discuss plans later at the Zimms' condo.

Back at The Star, Zero's stalker came looking for him, and with her French accent, said, "Darlin' you avoid me. I brokenhearted."

"Dame Isabella, meet my wife."

"You break this heart."

"I'm sorry, love won me over."

Cloud was startled. Dick and Dora, amused, were

trying not to laugh or even smile.

"I'm star, famous and beautiful. I do not know how you want do this to our love."

Zero, nearly speechless, stood up and hugged the once famous lady. "I know you will find someone else much more deserving of you."

Glaring at Cloud, the distressed and equally determined lady told her, "I will be watching two of you. I do not trust what you tell me."

Dick whispered to Dora, "Now this is something our bookie friend should make a bet on."

Chapter Twenty-Nine

Mission Anyone?

"All you have are theories. No facts. No evidence." Dick was being adamant.

"So, Zero, you're suggesting you and Buzz follow Kody Rothstein for a couple of days. Dora and Cloud would take on Jane Kohl and I would be in charge of Benjamin Rothstein?"

"Exactly," replied Zero and Cloud, both smug and smiling.

"Are you crazy? Any or all of them could be killers. I say we talk to the sheriff."

Dora loved it all.

"Dick, Cloud and I look innocent enough."

"I love you, my dear, but there is nothing innocent looking about you two stalking someone."

Standing at the bar in his living room, ready to pour himself another drink, aware from the beginning he was not going to win this battle Dick declared, "Fine. Only if we have some ground rules."

"Like what, dear?" Dora giving him her most charming and insincere smile and he knew it.

"Keep cell phones on at all times and stay in regular contact with each other."

"Done."

"Meet back here at nine each evening while we are doing this nonsense sleuthing. We'll have dinner delivered."

"Done. And what if we go back out after dinner?"

"Then we check in with each other every couple hours."

Zero told them about the plans and asked Buzz to meet him late the next morning. "I'll fill you in on the rest in the car."

Dora and Cloud made their plans to call Jane the next day.

Dick sat knowing none of this was going to be as simple as they were making it out to be.

For Dick and Dora Zimmerman, their sense of justice was driven by lessons learned in their youth and practiced in their careers. Long ago, they agreed that the real villains are those who teach and encourage people to hate and do evil.

Benjamin had certainly been that to his only son, Kody.

But someone had instilled it in Benjamin.

Kody had a grandfather who was a wiseguy. He'd never met him.

His father certainly had known him and what lessons he learned from grandpa were not those off television shows like *The Brady Bunch* or *Leave it to Beaver*. His lessons were more like the bad guys in the *Untouchables*.

Wiseguy connections were usually secret. There were secret ones that would eventually shock even Benjamin.

Chapter Thirty

No More

After the rain it became unusually hot for winter in Vegas.

On the Strip, gamblers looking for a score were moving a bit slower. Hookers waited until the sun went down to look for johns.

Glenn Erickson sat in his usual booth at the back of the small coffee shop off the Strip, so he could watch who came and went.

"Coffee, Sam. I'm waiting for my brother."

There were regulars who came here daily. Glenn came on his days off. He liked to be where people were not out to con or scam one another. Even when life had been tough for some of them, they showed a lot more dignity than those who came regularly to The Tuxedo Café and others places like it on the Strip.

"Glenn, I need your help." That was his brother Gordi's greeting.

"Nice to see you too. I got you out on bail for brandishing that gun and being drunk. You'll have to be in court next week."

Glenn could tell his brother was strung out in more ways than one.

"Yeah, yeah. I got a bigger problem. I borrowed money from some guys who said if I can't pay it back by end of the week, they'll take me for a ride to the desert."

"How much do you owe?" asked Glenn.

"Ten grand."

"What were you into?"

"I don't need no lectures from ya. I need the money and fast." Gordi was slurring his words the more he talked.

Glenn was fed up. "What did you do with the money?"

"I invested it."

"You invested it? What the hell did you invest it in?"

"Stuff."

Glenn knew the money was mostly for drugs and booze. He asked, "Are you mixed up in something with Kody Rothstein?"

Getting more anxious and looking around the coffee shop, Gordi Erickson shook as he stood up, shouting, "To hell with you and your money."

Glenn watched him walk, more like stumble, out of the café. He knew there was nothing more he could do to help his brother.

"Sam, I need another cup of coffee. Extra strength. I do believe I'm unemployed."

Chapter Thirty-One

Buzz and Zero Sneaking Around

"I've seen them half a dozen times at The Underworld Saloon," Buzz told Zero, who was driving there in the late afternoon.

"Anyone else ever with them?"

"Once I saw a young woman meet them there. Bartender seems friendly with them."

"He drives a red sports car. I don't see it here today." Buzz was familiar with this place and its patrons. "Let's wait inside for a little while, ask the bartender if he was here early. If he doesn't show up we'll come back tomorrow."

The next day a little after four in the afternoon, Kody walked into The Underworld Saloon and sat in the back booth. Within ten minutes, Gordi joined him. For the second day in a row, Buzz and Zero had made it a point to sit in the booth right in front of the back booth. The day before, after being shown a photo of Kody, the bartender said, "The guy you're asking about...not here today. But he and his buddy always sit in the last booth."

Behind them, the two younger men were whispering. Zero stretched his legs and leaned back against the booth trying to hear at least some of their conversation.

"We can get lots of money for doing this," Kody was saying to Gordi.

"From who?"

"My father."

"You hate him. And what about me? My brother's refused to give me any more money."

"I do hate him. He's disgusting, but he said he'll pay both of us to help him with a big problem. Hey, know what? Gordi, we get this money, maybe we should go to Mexico for some fun and broads."

After they left, arms around each other, laughing and totally drunk, planning to be big men somewhere or other, Zero called the bartender over and ordered another drink, mostly so he could pretending to be joking. "Crazy guys, are they always loud and drunk?"

"Just about."

Zero noticed the bartender hadn't looked at him, as if he was part of their scheme, or certainly something more complicated than serving patrons their drinks.

In the meantime, Dora and Cloud had put their stalking plan in motion.

"Jane's husband was found dead on the plane from New York to Las Vegas, then there was the public fight with Rothstein at The Black Tie bar. Cloud, I think she's hiding plenty," said Dora while she and Cloud had breakfast together.

"I say we invite her for a cocktail. We've met a few times in the past."

At four that afternoon, Dora and Cloud, dressed casually, met Jane at The Parasol Up Bar in the Wynn Las Vegas, known for its craft cocktails and beautiful atmosphere. It was a place where if money could talk, it would.

The three women discussed fashion and romance, not murder. They expressed sympathy about Jane's husband, watched her unemotional reaction and afterwards carefully followed her to the same bar where Buzz and Zero had just seen Kody and Gordi.

"Think they all know each other?"

They had rented a car for the day in order to do their sleuthing and spying. Dora was driving carefully to stay far enough behind, hoping not to be noticed.

At The Underworld Saloon, they watched Jane rush over and hug a man getting out of his car. It was Krupe.

"Can't be a coincidence," said Cloud, taking photos of them with her cell phone. Later when everyone met to report in it was agreed something strange, maybe even sinister, was going on at that bar.

That would prove to be an understatement.

Chapter Thirty-Two

Tempted

"Can we meet tomorrow?"

"Sure. How about seven at The Underworld Saloon? I have a job downtown that starts at nine."

They had been sleeping together off and on for several years, always at his place. Her explanation was it was better that way. Now Jane sounded desperate.

"He's threatening me."

"Why would he do that?"

"I have compromising photos of him."

"Have you shown them to him?"

"Only a couple."

"Jane, what do you want me to do? I really don't understand what's going on here." Krupe was bewildered by her behavior. She wasn't making any sense. He knew she was referring to Benjamin Rothstein. This wasn't the first time she expressed concern about his attitude toward her.

"I don't know."

"Maybe give him the photos and he'll leave you alone."

"I can't." Jane was into fake tears, same as she did for her father when she was a child so he would give her whatever it was she wanted.

"Want me to talk to him?"

"He won't listen to talk. Somebody needs to threaten him."

Krupe put his arm around her, kissed her on the cheek and said, "Jane, I adore you, but that's not something I can do."

"Maybe someone you know." She was playing him better than he played his drums...so she thought. He may have adored her, but he wasn't stupid.

He had a bad feeling, especially in light of her husband's recent murder. His protective instincts were kicking in and he had no intention of being her fall guy.

Jane, turned, kissed him passionately on the lips, then showed him one of the photos.

"Wow. That's quite a sight."

Giggling and acting all cutesy, she said, "I know. Maybe if he sees someone else has copies of these he'll stay away from me."

"How did you get photos like this?"

"What difference does it make?"

"You've been sleeping with him, haven't you?"

"Only before I knew you, not since. Honest."

Krupe inched away from her.

"What's wrong?"

"You."

Jane moved closer to him, seductive, trying to tempt him.

"I'm tempted, sweetheart, but not to go to Rothstein. I'm tempted to go to the sheriff and tell him what you're up to. You're quite the babe, aren't you? A murdered husband, threatening another man with photos, and hoping to con me into getting involved in some mess you've created."

Reaching over to slap him, Krupe grabbed her hand, pushed it away, and got up, leaving while the lovely lady was shouting, "Go to hell!"

"I fear that's where you're headed, love."

After seeing them both leave, Dora went into the bar, slipped the bartender a fifty dollar bill who then told her about their shouting and the slap.

"Hey, this is Vegas," she said when Cloud expressed surprise at Dora giving him fifty.

"Well, in Albuquerque, a ten can get you answers."

Dora told Cloud, "The bartender heard her make a phone call for someone to meet her tomorrow. Didn't hear who or where."

"I don't like this place, feels bad, and the night sky is strangely dark. My ancestors would tell us it is a sign to stay away from here."

"You're trembling."

"Dora, let's go back to The Star for a drink."

Chapter Thirty-Three

Dick and Benjamin

"Dick, what do you want?"

"What's going on? You seem on edge and angry. Benjamin, I've known you a long time. Maybe it would help to talk."

"You bet I'm angry. I'm angry at my screw up of a son, my bitch of a wife, and my business associates cheating me. Is that enough for you?"

Dick was sure most of it was not the truth. They were in Benjamin's suite having coffee, the late morning sky much brighter than the mood in the room.

"I saw your son in the café the other morning. He was yelling and grabbing one of the young ladies who works in your casino."

"See? Screw up." Rothstein was setting his son up as a fall guy. Ruthless and cruel, he didn't care about anyone but himself. "I think he's done something terrible, and he won't listen to me."

"Have you told the sheriff?"

"Hell no, I can't do that to my own son."

Sure, right, thought Dick. "What about your other situations? Can I help in any way?"

"Probably not. They're my burdens to bear."

"What if we both talked to the sheriff?"

Benjamin stood up and shouted, "Damn it, I told you no."

"No need to get upset." Dick watched, wondering how dangerous the man might be.

"Dick, get out or I'll have you thrown out." Benjamin looked crazed, red-faced and sweaty, shouting, pacing, threatening.

"He's blaming everyone else for his troubles," Dick said to the others at the update meeting.

Dora asked, "Do you think he's murdered anyone?"

"Maybe. Anything is possible. We still have no evidence."

Zero, stood by the window, concerned. "From the sounds of it, he could become very dangerous."

"Probably already is," Cloud commented.

"Maybe we should talk to the sheriff." Dick became more and more concerned.

"Give us a couple more days," Dora asked. Everyone quietly agreed.

"But only a couple more days," Dick stated firmly as he poured himself another drink.

Dora and Cloud told the others about following Jane as dinner arrived from a nearby Chinese restaurant.

Zero joked, "It's ten o'clock, do you know where your murderers are?"

In bed after midnight, Dick was reading the *New York Times,* and Dora was watching an old black and white film. She gave Dick a shove. "This movie stars our New York condo neighbor. This is the famous noir film he told us he appeared in years ago." Dora remembered once more things he had told her.

"Those films and many of their directors had a major influence on the industry, and because of some of them mystery stories became increasingly popular. These films, always in black and white, set a mood with the pace and the characters. Stories were usually in big cities, dark places, dim lighting, sometimes, bad weather and lots of shadows cast on walls and stairways. What about romantic scenes? Of course, there were romantic scenes and many of the films had great lighthearted moments with funny one-liners."

The film over, shadows from outside lights flickering through their blinds, a sleepy Dick mumbled a warning. "Dora, there's quite a few bad people involved with Jane Kohl. You and Cloud need to be careful."

Chapter Thirty-Four

Logical

"It's illogical."

"Who are you, Spock?"

Zero was doing his imitation of the famous quote as his friends stared at him like he'd lost his marbles. Inside the Zimms' apartment discussing what they had, or more like had not, for evidence, had them feeling as if they were getting nowhere.

"Maybe because we should leave this to the sheriff," Dick said, still not thrilled with the back alley stalking.

"Stop it, darling. We just need to think this through. As Zero suggests, logically."

"Fine. Let's begin with the dead man on the plane. Do you recall anything about his demeanor or body language? Did he talk to you at all?"

"His face was bloated and flushed, his eyes were closed and he was leaning back in the seat. I didn't talk to him."

"How did his briefcase fall?"

"It had been on his lap. I noticed it there when I got up earlier. It must have fallen from his lap into the aisle. It made a noise when it landed. That's when I first poked

113

him to let him know his case had fallen. I waited a minute or so, touched him gently again and he fell over. I was pretty sure he was dead. His wasn't the first dead body I've seen."

"What happened next?"

"Well..."

"Well, the key sort of fell onto the floor from of his briefcase."

"Did it or didn't it?"

Zero burst out laughing. Cloud stared at him. "You grabbed it out of his case."

"Not exactly. The key fell out."

"Dora, you're a delight. We'll do five years for tampering with evidence in a murder investigation." Zero was unusually sarcastic, but this was real trouble for them if the sheriff found out.

"It was on the floor, I didn't put it there."

"Did anyone see you pick up the key?"

"I don't think so. The flight attendants were back in coach."

Cloud asked, "What about the flask? Did it fall out of his briefcase?"

"No, it was on his lap."

"Wait, he was mumbling. His words were slurred, probably from his being poisoned. He was repeating 'code, code,' but—"

"Meaning Kody?" Dick gave Dora a hug.

Buzz, listening to everyone, knew the game was more than afoot. It was moving fast. "Sure, Boss, but why?"

"Buzz, I need you and Zero to talk to the boys who found the icebox in the desert and ask them about what they saw."

"How do we know who they are?" Zero stood up, realizing Cloud was staring at his orange and purple polka dot suspenders.

"Hey, these are hip and happening."

Smiling he turned to Buzz. "You know how to find them?"

"Damn straight. After they spoke with Deputy Turner, they were back in their dorm bragging about it."

An hour later at the university dorm, Buzz found the boys. "I need information from you two, and don't give me any B.S."

"Are you with the police?"

"No, but if you lie to me, I can give you more trouble than they can."

"Hey, we didn't do anything except find the icebox and the body in it."

"Did you see anyone else while you were out there?"

"That time of night? No way."

"Did you know the woman stuffed in it?"

"Nope."

"Did you see anything on the ground around the icebox?"

One of the boys looked at the other and said quietly, "We picked up a few casino chips. They probably fell out of someone's pocket."

"Do you have them?"

"Yeah, we've been afraid to do anything with them. Figured the sheriff would put us in jail if he knew we kept them. Are you going to tell him?"

Taking the chips, he said, "You two get to class and

be quiet about what you found."

Chapter Thirty-Five

Criminal Acts

"Can you loan me some money?"

"If...would you spy on your father for me?"

"Gladly."

For six years it had been a mutually beneficial relationship based on hate and greed. They hated Benjamin Rothstein.

Jane Kohl knew how to use Kody Rothstein's hate for his father. Her money and his need for it was a match made in heaven...or more likely hell.

"I heard him trying to hire someone. He mentioned your name, but the person on other end hung up on him. My father was cursing him."

"Has your father met with any of the casino syndicate recently?"

"No, but he's been talking to one guy a lot, never seems friendly."

"Does he have any idea you're listening to his conversations?"

"Nah, in general he ignores me, thinks I'm busy on the computer."

"I want to know if he meets with any one of them. I gave you their names."

"Sure thing."

Kody brought her information he heard, she gave him money. But a few weeks earlier Kody called Jane with something disturbing.

"He's been on the phone a lot recently with your husband, Zachary."

"What do they talk about?"

"Last call this morning, my father said something about paying him a lot of money and would cancel his gambling debts."

"Could you hear what he wanted him to do?"

"No. Bu the told him it would happen here in Las Vegas."

"Can you follow him for a few days? See what he's up to?"

"Sure. I could use some money."

"I'll deposit some into your account in the morning."

"Why don't you ask your husband?"

"Not a chance. But you gave me an idea, Kody. I'll need to check the papers on his desk."

Careless and inept, Zachary had scribbled a note. *Jane, Rothstein, Vegas.* She knew that couldn't be anything good.

Two days later, Kody had called sounding scared. "Jane, my father went to the bus station to rent a locker and put a manila envelope in it. I went back the next day, and I managed to get a key."

"Stop panicking. Slow down, breathe. What did you find?" Jane was shouting, but Kody was having a panic attack. They started when he was a young teenager.

Kody and his mother had been bullied by his father for years. Her saving grace was when he wanted a divorce so he could marry Deidre.

She signed the papers, walked away with not much money and lots of gratitude to be rid of him. She told Kody, "Stay away from him. He'll destroy you."

By the time he was nineteen it was too late. On drugs, dropping out of college, his father's money holding power over him. Along with the panic attacks it was one of the consequences of his life with a bully and a brute.

Asking him to do this or that, taking care of this or that. Kody's father was constantly dangling money as payment for favors he asked. More like demanded.

He had been doing bad things for his father for years. Slapping around employees, cutting the brake lines on cars of gamblers who owed him money, lying to people who were looking for his father...by the time he was in his thirties it was routine.

He remembered as a young boy hiding in a small closet in his bedroom when he would hear him and his mother fighting. He put on head phones to listen to music, waited for a couple hours, praying for quiet, for his father's car to be gone. His mother would refuse to talk to him, going into her bedroom, shutting the door, shutting him out.

Dick and Dora had met dozens of flawed people like the Rothsteins and Kohls. Some unethical, some sociopaths, even a psychopath or two, he as an attorney, she as a judge.

Over the years they'd had conversations about these types of people they'd met along the way. "Misery and brutal behavior passed on from generation to generation. Many such awful stories. It's a courageous person who finally says enough and changes their family dynamics."

When Kody finally calmed down he whispered to Jane, as if someone might hear him, "He had a photo of you in the envelope, money and a gun. There was a typed note on the photo. It said 'kill her.'"

"Couple of S.O.B.'s. Kody, go home. I know how to handle this."

Jane knew her housekeeper was always glad to earn extra money. Together they arranged the arsenic murder of her husband.

"No one will be able to blame me. I'll be in Las Vegas."

Chapter Thirty-Six

Sheriffs and Sleuths

"They've been too quiet," Sheriff Foster barked at his deputy. "I've a bad feeling they're investigating Zachary Kohl's murder."

They meaning Dick and Dora.

"Maybe they're enjoying the great weather we're having," Turner said without looking at his boss. He knew better, word on the street according to a couple of his personal confidential informants was it's exactly what they were doing.

"Turner, don't give me such a load of bull. I know you hear things. Keep an eye on them. Get one of the other officers to help. Maybe we can prevent them from causing us too much trouble."

Sheriff Foster also spoke with a New York detective several times about Zachary Kohl's murder and his not-so-charming wife.

"She's a busy lady, affairs with numerous men."

"Including her housekeeper?"

"Especially her housekeeper. The night doorman who once enjoyed accommodations in upstate New York at Sing Sing was only too glad to tell us about her."

"Still can't find the housekeeper?"

121

"Doorman told us same day her husband left for Vegas, he came out, got into a taxi and told the driver to take him to the International Terminal at Kennedy Airport."

"Did he have luggage?"

"Small carry-on bag."

"Any chance of finding out what airline or where he was going?"

"Checking on that now, Sheriff. We'll let you know soon as we find out anything."

"Probably won't matter. Chances are he's never coming back." Foster thanked him adding, "Think she paid him to poison her husband?"

"From the sounds of it, anything is possible with her."

◆ ♣ ♥ ♠

Foster ordered a couple police officers to follow Jane, now that she was in Vegas. They reported seeing her with Kody Rothstein and another time having drinks with Dora Zimmerman and an Indian lady.

"She's Zero's friend. They're up to something, damn it. Keep a watch on them. Where did Jane meet with Kody?"

"At a bar outside the city limits. They were having a heated conversation. She took his hand, he looked all anxious and she was acting all caring."

"Lady only cares about herself." With that, Sheriff Foster called Dick Zimmerman. "Meet me for coffee. I want to know what you can tell me about Benjamin Rothstein."

Chapter Thirty-Seven

Grandpa

In a small café near police headquarters, Dick sat sipping coffee telling Sheriff Foster what he knew about Benjamin. A story he had been told by a mutual friend years ago, the rest he learned by reading about his family history thanks to the many stories written about the Mob.

"His father, Kody's grandfather, was involved with the Mob." Dick leaned back in the booth with its deep tan leather cushions looking around the immaculate café filled with locals, especially from the Las Vegas Police Department. There was a counter with eight stools also in the same color leather, half dozen booths and a few smaller tables down the middle of the restaurant.

"Did you meet his father?"

"No. He and Benjamin parted ways when he left home at fifteen He told his father to drop dead and took a baseball bat his father used on him a few times and smashed him in the legs with it."

"Stopped him from going after him," the sheriff commented.

"Exactly. Apparently his mother told him to run as far away as he could. The oldest of three boys, he had taken the brunt of his father's brutal behavior."

"Where did he go?"

"Sheriff, he came here, to Vegas. Hitchhiked from south Chicago. Had an uncle he met a few times who was nice to him."

The conversation was interrupted several times, officers stopping by to tell something to the sheriff. Dick noticed how respectful they were of this man who had served this city for so many years.

"You must have heard of his uncle, Izzy Rothstein. His father's younger brother was making a lot of money in Vegas. He saw a hunger in Benjy, what had driven him, the same kind of hunger he himself had for money and power."

"Sure, I heard of him. Some of his best friends are on the wall of infamy at The Mob Museum. Have you been there?"

"Not yet."

"Dick you should add it to your To Do list."

"Brady, I don't have a To Do list."

"Top of mine is to convince you to spend your winters elsewhere, make some other police department crazy instead of mine."

Both men laughed. It had been a running joke for the past several years.

"At any rate, Benjy was accepted as his uncle's nephew. Ran small errands at first, after a couple years they had him collecting money owed them. Uncle Izzy paid for him to go to college, wanted him to have a degree, be educated. He told him, 'I wants you should be able to mingle with rich people and politicians. It's good for business.'"

He met Izzy's buddies who hung out at a small

store beneath a dance studio downtown. They taught him how to be a tough guy. When he turned eighteen they took him shopping for clothes to fit the image they were creating. At twenty-two he graduated college with a degree in business, a degree in street smarts from his uncle and plenty of connections with his uncle's friends."

"Mob friends?" the sheriff interrupted.

"Mostly, and some good looking lady friends."

"My source told me Izzy talked about some inside stories he probably shouldn't have, including about the Saint Valentine's Day Massacre."

"Dick, you gotta be kidding. By the way your cell phone is beeping for the third time."

"No big deal, I'll call them back when we're finished." He knew his wife and others were snooping and sleuthing, not something he wanted to share with the Las Vegas sheriff.

"Didn't that massacre happen in a garage in Chicago?"

"Sure did. Izzy told his nephew his father was involved although he wasn't one of the actual shooters. Maybe it's true, maybe just a story, either way Benjamin Rothstein grew up with these stories, a brutal father and gangster uncle. I read about his connection to his uncle and others known as wise guys or made men. There's a fun conversation for another time."

Foster's phone was beeping with a text message. *Urgent, need you back at headquarters soon as possible.*

"Dick, I have to go. By the way what happened to those two?"

"Dead. Father dropped dead of a heart attack when he was in his fifties. Uncle had a problem with the Mob and he was found in the desert a few years later. Benjamin got married, and opened his hotel and casino with some help from various investors."

Getting up to leave, putting money down for the bill, almost daring Dick to try and stop him, he said, "One last question, at least for now. Do you think Benjamin is capable of murder?"

"Yes. Absolutely, thanks to dear ole grandpa's legacy." Dick burst out laughing and got up to walk out with Sheriff Foster.

"Next cup of coffee is on me."

"Damn right it is." Foster turned and went to face more trouble in sin city.

Chapter Thirty-Eight

Beyond Help

G lenn Erickson, still concerned, called his brother. As angry with him as he was, his heart ached for him, for the man he could have been without drugs and booze.

"What are you doing running around with Kody Rothstein? The two of you are up to no good."

"Whadya mean? Whadya care? You won't help me. You walked out on me so leave me alone." Words slurring, Gordi was drunk again.

"A couple employees at The Black Tie complained to me about being threatened by Kody."

"So? Nothin' to do with me."

"A female employee has been reported missing."

"I don't know anything about it."

"Does Kody?"

"How should I know?"

"People I know see you with him a lot."

"Yeah, we hang out together, talk about getting out of this place."

"Really, Gordi, where would the two of you go?" Glenn said, sarcastic and annoyed.

"California, maybe LA."

"What would you do there? You hardly work here."

"I could get a job as a bartender. Hey, I might even get discovered and be in the movies."

Glenn feared the only thing anyone would discover about Gordi Erickson is he was a drunk and a fool, and possibly worse.

"Me and him got plans."

"To do what?"

"None of your business, big brother."

"Remember, you get in trouble, I can't help you anymore."

"His father can, even told us he would."

"Gordi, believe me, I know the man. He's lying. He wants him to do something he won't do himself."

"Yeah, well he gave him money. So did some lady friend of his."

"What lady?"

"He wouldn't tell me, and I don't care."

"Again, I'm asking you, what do they want you to do?"

"Again, I'm telling you, I ain't saying."

Gordi hung up. In his gut Glenn knew both of them were beyond help. *Who is the woman? What does she want?* he wondered to himself.

Kody continued to be in the middle of two dangerous and unscrupulous people who were using his weakness and vulnerability as a means of trying to save their own lives and reputations.

Life has a way of biting at you unexpectedly and Benjamin Rothstein and Jane Kohl were taking chances by gambling on their futures with a couple of losers. No way this would pay off well.

Zero could have told them they needed better odds.

Chapter Thirty-Nine

Frankie Socks

"See what you can find out about Jane Kohl. You'll need to get into her apartment. I'll send the details to you." Dick had called Frankie Socks in Manhattan. Only one other person had Frankie's number and they had just spent the night together.

"Am I looking for something in particular?"

"Anything showing what she may have been up to recently."

"Like murder?"

"Yes. And Frankie, the sooner the better."

Frankie Socks was able to leave the Witness Protection Program after twenty years, thanks to the deaths of those who had threatened him for being a rat. Thanks to Dick Zimmerman who helped him enter the program, stayed in touch and told him one day, "Come home."

It was a peculiar relationship, a top Manhattan attorney and a Mob criminal. Dick and Dora had discussed it over the years, "I like the guy. He got a bad break being raised by a family of crooks and murderers."

"You're just a softy, dear." Dick knew Dora's condescending tone. As a judge she was known for being fair, but also tough.

"Come on Dora, you know when it came to his being a witness against the Mob he was a standup guy."

"True."

"I put away many Mob connections thanks to his testimony."

"That's correct, dear."

The conversation would go on like this usually ending with Dick giving Dora a hug or a kiss on the cheek, or more romantic overtures.

"He's been a big help since he's been back in Manhattan, even recently helped us catch those murderers."

"Yes, dear."

Dick couldn't help grinning, admiring her, thinking *Even when there was that damn voice.*

He would tell her not to use it on him. Dora would smile or shrug her shoulders.

"Yes, dear."

Frankie watched Jane's apartment building for a few hours wanting to get a feel for the place. He sat in his friend's car. It was too cold in New York to be hanging outside anywhere. He was remembering the last time he did this type of work, for the Mob. It got him sent to what felt like Siberia when he entered the Witness Protection Program.

Shaking off those unpleasant memories, late in the afternoon he went in. He handed the front desk manager two one hundred dollar bills.

"Jane Kohl's apartment?"

Frankie Socks hadn't lost his touch. For another hundred the manager slipped him a key to her place, commenting, "She's a nasty lady."

Dick knew Frankie had plenty of money when he came back to New York. He wisely never asked him where it came from.

After less than twenty minutes, he unlocked a desk drawer in her apartment and found a sealed envelope marked *Police*. Jane had no idea it was there. Her former housekeeper and lover, who killed her husband at her request, put it there after she left for Las Vegas.

Jane Kohl and I have been sleeping together for the past several years. Recently she hired me to poison Zachary Kohl's flask. At the bottom was his signature, bold and dated.

Under the note were sensational photos of Benjamin Rothstein. Sensational was an understatement.

Pulling out his cell phone, he called Dick. "I got stuff you're going to wanna see."

It seemed to Dick the stone-faced Frankie Socks was really enjoying all this. "Send it overnight to me at The Star, thanks."

Frankie still had the makings of a wiseguy.

Dick had a number of conversations with Socks over the years about wiseguys and being a made man.

Buzz also had told Dick and Dora about what was called the good old days according to the Mob. "Wiseguys and made men ruled the downtown and had juice, meaning power, in the casinos along the Strip. Benjamin's father had plenty of juice but never became a made man. You had to be Italian."

"I understand you had to kill someone to be accepted." Dora shook her head in disgust.

"You've seen the movies."

Dick chimed in, "I for one love those movies, old and new ones. Each one attempt to show some element of humanity about some of the characters even with all the violence and murders involving them."

"I know there have been stories making bad guys

look like heroes, but they're still bad guys even if they had families and gave money to good causes. That money came from illegal, often brutal activities." Dora was fully on her soapbox.

"Dora, I'm only telling you what it meant. How it got to be. I wasn't part of it." Buzz was feeling a bit defensive and to be honest a little annoyed.

"You're right, I'm sorry. I do get going when I hear about crimes and times that hurt so many people. What was the reason for becoming part of all this criminal activity?"

"Acceptance. Friendships. A need to feel a sense of belonging, for many it became their family. Along with it came money and power. The Mob had a huge network that included politicians and business leaders. They kept people in line through fear and threats often ending in murder."

Dick reminded them, "Many were ruthless like Albert Anastasia. He was head of Murder Inc. and loved to kill people. I understand you can see his and many others' pictures and stories at The Mob Museum."

Buzz sat back in his chair. They had been out to dinner when the talk, not unexpectedly, turned to murder and mayhem leading to the subject of the Mob, made men and wiseguys who thought they were above the law.

Little did Dick or anyone else think they would see that Wall of Infamy in The Mob Museum in the near future.

Chapter Forty

The Mustache

His birthday party had been planned since last year. It was what Dora did each year for "My Man," as she worded the invitation.

My Man is turning another year older. Join us for a casual dinner supplemented by drink, fun and frolic. No gifts, no RSVP required. Below was the date, cocktails to begin at eight and the place, their condo at The Star. She signed them *Love Dora.*

The guest list included people from all walks of Las Vegas life, some reputable, a few not so much. They were also from the police department, political life, the university and even some last minute guests, one of those being Jane Kohl.

Zero and Cloud arrived early. "We're here just in case."

"In case what?" Dick was busy setting up the bar in the corner of the living room.

"Any one tries to kill anyone else. Anything can happen at one of your gatherings."

Dick looked up and saw Zero dressed like a gangster from the twenties, including spats and a mustache pasted on his face.

Cloud had no comment. Dick was never surprised at what Zero might wear.

Next to the bar were several tall windows facing toward neon signs blinking off and on in true Vegas style, as always day and night, calling for gamblers to play at their casinos.

"Dick, darling I'll have a glass of champagne," Dora shouted from the bedroom.

"Dick, darling, me too," mimicked Zero.

Cloud, with her arm around Zero, said, "Oh yes, darling, me too."

"Bar is set up. You're all on your own. I need to dress for this birthday bash or Dora will be most displeased to have me attend in my robe."

Dora came out of the bedroom wearing a beautiful lilac evening dress, lace on top with a satin skirt. Hugging her as he walked past to go change, he simply said, "Beautiful."

"I love you too, dear. Happy birthday."

"Oh and feel free to ignore Zero's attire, he's pretending to be a wiseguy tonight."

By half past eight two bartenders began serving drinks non-stop for several hours and all levels of conversation were taking place on a variety of topics. There were discussions and disagreements on politics, casino corruption, entertainment choices and life in Las Vegas, including murder. Of course.

By nine their long dining room table had been covered with a white linen tablecloth, an all white orchid flower arrangement in the center and large white candles at each end. Platters of delicious food from shrimp to lobster salad, meat dishes, salads and ultimately delicious desserts appeared until well after midnight with plenty of wine and champagne. There was no birthday cake as demanded by Dick.

Some guests came for an hour, before they went off to other plans. Others stayed for the entire evening. A few came late. Jane Kohl was one of them. Zero and Buzz watched as Benjamin started to walk towards her.

Jane Kohl had shown up in that same tight, sexy black dress and winked at Benjamin, making him even more furious.

Sheriff Foster, an invited guest, caught Dick's glance at Buzz to intervene before Benjamin could create a problem.

"Sir, Dick was hoping he could have a word with you."

"Get out of my way. I need to talk to someone." Clearly agitated, Benjamin could not get past Buzz blocking his way.

"Fine. I'm leaving. No way I'm staying in the same room as that bitch."

"What bitch would that be, sir?"

"Get out of my way. Now."

With that Benjamin Rothstein stormed off leaving Jane Kohl delighted with the impact of her presence on Benjy.

Sheriff Foster saw it all and in minutes cornered Dick. "What's with separating those two?"

"May I ask what two you mean, Officer?"

"Lovely party, Dick. Cut the double talk." Foster was not to be deterred. He figured they knew more about Benjamin and Jane and the recent murders.

"Tomorrow. We'll talk at the poker game."

Foster texted his officers in one of two police cars downstairs, "Let me know where Rothstein goes. Kohl is still here. Follow her when she leaves."

In less than ten minutes, he got a response. "Sir, he picked up a hooker on Fremont and is heading to The Black Tie."

"Stay there. Let me know if he leaves."

Meantime Jane had settled down next to a politician who she helped get elected with large donations and shared sexual interest. That was Jane.

It was three in the morning. Dick and Dora were stretched on their sofa. Everyone had left including the caterers.

"Lovely party, Dora, thank you."

"Well, yes, except for her."

Her meant Dame Isabella who had rushed into the party around after nine wearing her finest fashions and jewelry, and grabbed Zero to claim him for her own. "You are mine, I tell you. She no good for you."

Buzz had taken her gently by the arm and walked her back to her own place.

As for Zero and Cloud, they had moved from friends to lovers.

In Albuquerque, Zero had told her a little about himself. "In my forties I opened a pool hall. It had a backroom where friendly poker games took place and often well-known members of the city life came to play. I was a bookie to the city's wealthier citizens and most of them thought nothing of losing thousands at a time."

"And now?"

"Getting older it's important to have a hobby, stay

busy."

In Cloud's hotel room, Zero slipped off his grey leather loafers, showing his purple and yellow polka dot socks.

She was keenly and happily aware he was making himself comfortable.

"When Dick and Dora are in New York, I am too. Same for Las Vegas. We've known each other for many years. They helped me legally and stood by me during a difficult time when family members caused me to lose a restaurant and bar I owned."

It was Cloud now making herself comfortable, taking off her three-inch heels, stretching her bare legs out on the sofa.

Walking over to her, his heart pounded. This was a big step for Zero. Cloud knew it and understood because it was difficult for her as well.

Zero the Bookie had taken a lot of bets and gambles in his lifetime, and now he was taking a chance on romance. Not an easy thing to do when you're far past youth. Still, passion is present at all ages, even if it appears differently than how it does in younger years.

If this was a movie it was time to fade to black.

As for Dick and Dora, nearly everyone agreed the hit of the party was the black paste-on mustache handed to guests as they arrived, thanks do Dora's enduring sense of humor.

Dick agreed it was pretty darn funny as he turned to see Dora with the mustache stuck on her lip. Pulling her toward him, their hug continued into the bedroom.

"Hey, older people enjoy some lovin too," Dick and

Dora once commented to Zero when he was making fun of them.

He wasn't going to make fun of them anymore. Seems he was finding it all too true.

Chapter Forty-One

Ladies Night Out

"We have tickets to The Nevada Ballet. A nice change from murders and mysteries while the men enjoy their poker night," Dora told Cloud. "It's performed at the Smith Center for Performing Arts in downtown Las Vegas."

This night was meant to be an escape from ugliness into a world of beauty.

The evening was full of surprises.

Walking in, Deidre Rothstein seemed to appear out of nowhere, hugging Dora hello, meeting Cloud, rambling on about what a jackass Benjamin was and on and on until it was time to find their seats and then she seemed to disappear.

Sitting halfway back from the stage, Cloud noticed her "competition," Dame Isabella in handicapped seating upstairs, giving her dirty looks. Ignoring her, Cloud's Native American upbringing, lessons on listening to your instincts, following your inner voice had her sensing something about this evening felt strange.

"Dora, have you known Deidre a long time?"

"Yes, years ago we socialized with her and Benjamin until Dick and I found it too unpleasant to be in their company. Always fighting or snapping at each other. After begging off a few times she stopped calling. Why?"

Dora in the short time she knew Cloud was aware this was not a frivolous woman or question for that matter. The house lights dimming, silence in the theatre, Cloud responded with a shrug of her shoulders and quietly offering a one word answer. "Strange."

It was a long performance with an intermission, a conversation related to the beauty of the dancers, Dora saying hello to a few people she knew, and finally following the crowd out of the theatre sometime after ten.

Cloud saw Deidre again. She began walking out with them, chatting about the ballet. It was as if all three were moving in slow motion, Deidre talking fast, Dora hardly commenting, Cloud putting her shoulder bag across her body, her protective instincts on full alert. Instincts and behaviors had served her well from her childhood and youth on the Indian Reservation to taunts at college to a career demanding caution and intelligence.

Dora put her arm through Cloud's feeling her tension. Asking only, "Anything wrong?"

Cloud shook her head no.

As they walked towards the line of Las Vegas taxi cabs waiting out front, an old, dirty white van pulled up, two men dressed in black with black masks jumped out shouting for everyone not to move, and pointing guns at their target. Later photos of Dora and Cloud would be found in the van with a huge red X across each one.

With onlookers stunned, Dora and Cloud were grabbed, and pulled into the van. The two women were kidnapped as they left the Smith Center

They were blindfolded with their hands tied, forced to the floor and warned not to talk. The driver and another man kept on their black hoods as they talked in whispers. Dora could still hear pieces of their conversation.

"Hurry, he's waiting for us."

"I am. We don't want to get caught speeding."

"Yeah well we need to get them out of this van."

Meantime there was plenty of chaos at the Center. Someone ran after the van and wrote down its make and license number and shouted, "Call the police." Someone else screamed and fainted. The crowd at the center was now in a hurry to leave, running to their cars, getting into a waiting taxi or walking away quickly. Fear had overtaken the night's beauty and no one felt safe. Deidre, who had been right next to Dora as they walked out, ran into the crowd.

One of the onlookers was Dame Isabella.

Dick was playing poker with Zero, Sheriff Foster and Buzz when he got the call from Deidre Rothstein. Sounding out of breath, she said, "Someone has kidnapped Dora and her friend Cloud in front of the Smith Center. Dick, it's Deidre Rothstein. I was there, I saw it happen."

Dick stood up, grabbed Zero and frantically shouted, "They've been kidnapped, I told you we should stop this!"

"Stop what? Who's been kidnapped?"

The sheriff's phone began ringing. "Turner get police to the Smith Center, talk to witnesses, and get a description of the suspect's vehicle. I'm on my way."

Dick and Zero went with Foster, jumped into the back of his police car and briefly told him about their sleuthing, stalking, and harassing. He would deal with their craziness later. Right now his top priority was finding the two abducted women safe and sound.

Sirens blaring, rushing through the streets, Vegas seemed to belong once again to the dark side, their surroundings surreal.

"I see two men jump out of white van and grab the women."

"Did you see what they looked like?" Deputy Turner had sat Dame Isabella down in the back seat of his patrol car.

"No. But I hear the tall one yell, 'Damn, Kody, lock your door.'"

Chapter Forty-Two

Kidnapped

F ools come in all sizes and ages, from many different lifestyles and from both wealth and poverty. Fools are dangerous. Their lack of good judgment can cause them to impulsively do harm.

Dora and Cloud listened to the whispering of a couple of such fools as they were driven away from the Smith Center.

"You did good."

"Yeah, you too."

"Got the key?"

"Sure do."

"When we get there we need to call in and find out what we're supposed to do with them."

"We should be there in about fifteen minutes."

Dora had worked in the criminal justice system long enough to realize these two had no idea what they were doing. The van soon stopped and they were taken out none too gently, and literally stuffed into the back seat of a very small car. There was more whispering as they heard the driver give the keys to someone else.

"How long do you want me to drive around in this piece of junk?"

"At least an hour, unless someone stops you," one of the kidnappers told him.

The other one shouted, irritated, "We need to get out of here now! We need to go before we're late!"

The dirty white van and the small car with the two women inside moved in opposite directions as Dora wondered *Late for what?*

After the sheriff and a dozen officers from the Las Vegas sheriff's department responded to the kidnapping call, Dame Isabella and other witnesses continued to be questioned about the kidnapping. Most of the answers were of little help.

"They wore black masks. The van drove off that way. No it was the other way. They were definitely younger. Well, not really old."

Dick knew five witnesses could say ten different things. His worry was palpable and his sensing this was far more complicated than it seemed would prove true.

There was no way the sheriff could have stopped Dick and Zero from going with him unless he shot them each in the foot. He was sorely tempted to do just that.

Rushing out after the poker game, Buzz had immediately called a few of his rather unorthodox friends for help. They knew their way around the seedier side of the city, those who hung out there, those who lived by their own rules and often died by them.

Dora had no doubt many people would be looking for her and Cloud. She was also sure Dick would be worried and surely angry that he went along with the whole sleuthing, snooping and harassing scheme. He was much more sensible than she when it came to wanting to get involved in a murder mystery. She was relentless. He was cautious. She was passionate, he was uneasy. Having prosecuted many bad guys he knew they could be vicious and vindictive.

Stuffed into the little car with no room to even move, Cloud sat silent, her purse still across her body. Dora's was lost on the floor of the van, and she willed her mind to wander to give her relief from the situation. Dora hoped they would be okay. Still, she remembered when she met with their famous noir film star and penthouse neighbor in New York before they went to Vegas.

"Dick thinks I go overboard in what he calls sleuthing. I find it difficult to let go of solving a problem."

"Or a crime."

"Yes, I'm afraid so," she replied. *Dora was fascinated by the person, and the room she was sitting in, as they talked. She liked him. He was interesting and at the same time interested in others.*

"Did you like your work?" he responded.

"Very much so. When it was over it was over. Times change. I'm fortunate to have had the experience."

"Still, you seem connected to all you did. The photos in here are wonderful and amazing reminders."

Dora walked around the room. On one wall were dozens of photos, many of other famous people she recognized.

"They are. Makes me happy to have those photos, to have had time with them."

"Did you learn a lot about the industry when you were involved?"

"Sure. The work is not all that complicated. It's probably similar to what you realized as a judge. People allow their ambitions or greed to make situations difficult and then they become complicated."

"They do, don't they? That and an almost outrageous sense of self can motivate the worst behaviors."

"Let me ask you a question."

"Okay." Dora was curious about him, why shouldn't he be curious about her.

"Why do you like what you do? You're retired as a judge still you continue in similar pursuits."

"Justice. The desire for fairness which is not always easy to accomplish"

He had looked at her with penetrating eyes questioning her response.

"Okay, well I guess I have a strong sense of adventure as well as justice. Getting older doesn't mean I have to live or act old. Not yet a least. Maybe there will be a time for being less involved. At least I believe I'll not feel any regret about living a less fulfilled life."

"You know you're a dichotomy of traits from what I can see."

"Such as? You don't think I'm going to leave here without your insight on that?"

"You're stubborn and confident. You have a heart full of love and probably gratitude while you're also extremely impatient."

"Is that such a bad thing?"

"Only when you allow it to lead you into trouble, which I suspect it has a number of times."

"True."

"Nevertheless, you know, you're not always as careful as you should be."

"Also true."

"I suspect you know it's very true. I also suspect it won't stop you in the future."

Dora laughed again as she got up to leave, thanking him

for his time. She didn't want to stay too long. He was no longer a young man, however, he still had a strength and vibrancy well into his nineties..

"*You're a wonderful role model.*" Dora smiled and leaned over to kiss him goodbye on the cheek, leaving a huge smile on his face.

Thinking about their conversation, yes she did have a flair for getting into troublesome situations.

The car suddenly stopped and Dora was back to the reality of being kidnapped.

Now what? wondered Dora.

Cloud thought, *Hope they don't take my purse, my gun is in it.*

Chasing after the van, weaving in and out of the busy traffic, passing the big hotels and casinos, The Venetian, Caesar's Palace, The Mirage, and other casinos on the Strip, the police caught up with the speeding white van. Finally stopping it outside of city limits, the driver's door was pulled open, and he was staring at guns. Police officers then pushed the driver to the ground and handcuffed him.

"It's a set-up. No one is inside." They had been chasing after the dirty white van meant to distract them from the real culprits.

"Where are the two women who were shoved into this van at the Smith Center?"

"How the hell do I know?"

"This van drove up there and grabbed them less than half an hour ago."

"Hey all I know is I was hired to drive this piece of junk and get it as far out of town as possible."

"Who hired you?"

The driver, nervous and scared, was about thirty

years old, wore dirty jeans and a t-shirt smelling of pot. "Some dude hangs out at a bar. Met him there a few times."

"What does he look like?"

"About forty, short, dark hair, gave me two hundred bucks to do this."

"Do you know his name?" The officer grabbed him even tighter.

"Hey, man, you're hurting me. I heard the other guy he hangs out with call him Kody."

"What kind of car are they in now?"

"Sheriff, the driver of the van said the two women were put into a red sports car driven by someone called Kody. He heard one of the two men ask something about the key to a museum."

The sheriff put out an all-points bulletin on Kody Rothstein's red sports car, stressing museum areas and parking lots.

Buzz was listening to the police monitor. He knew the car. Kody often drove it to The Underworld Bar.

The cross-dresser told Buzz, "You know he's pals with a guy who used to work at The Mob Museum, someone named Gordi. Before he realized I am who I am, he tried to pick me up."

"No kidding?"

"Yeah, I offered to meet him another time. He ran out screaming some obscenity."

"We're almost near the museum. I'll drive around the parking lots and side streets. You look for the car. We need to find these fools."

Four of Buzz's buddies responded to his messages for help, two Elvis impersonators, a cross dresser made up to look like Cher, and a wannabe Frank Sinatra. All on his speed dial for such emergencies, he picked them up in front of the Bellagio Hotel where they often gambled. They too had raced around the city looking for the van. Now they were pretty sure they knew where to find the red sports car and the two kidnapped women.

Calling Dick, he said, "Boss, I think they're at The Mob Museum. We're on our way there."

Listening to police calls, hearing about the van set up, Kody and his red sports car and now Dick's call about The Mob Museum, the sheriff was more than a little concerned.

"I don't like this. What are they going to do there? For smart people you're all pretty damn stupid."

Dick and Zero listened as the sheriff yelled at them for not letting him know what they were doing. "Are all of you nuts? Now Dora and Cloud have been kidnapped by what are a couple of loose cannons. There's no telling what they might do or who else is involved."

Panicked, there was nothing they could do, or say. Not yet. Not now.

Chapter Forty-Three

The Mob Museum

They were taken to the basement of The Mob Museum and tied to chairs obviously waiting for them. Gordi had once worked there as part of a cleaning crew and never returned his keys, telling them, "I lost them."

Taking up a full corner in Downtown Vegas, near Fremont Street, the sign across the front of the building stated, "National Museum of Organized Crime and Law Enforcement."

According to the museum website: Real stories are brought to life with engaging exhibits and unparalleled insights from those on the front lines of both sides of the battle. There's a wall of infamy, profiling the most notorious figures from more than one hundred years of mob history.

The displays of photos and relics from the Mob heyday to the FBI catching up with them, to the end of their glory and gory days covered the walls of the three floors dedicated to the history of underworld figures. It was filled with stories and history from the beginnings of mobsters such as the infamous Lucky Luciano, to events like the St. Valentine's Day massacre, to numerous arrests and convictions of many made men.

These men and a few women had ruled the city

and various Mob families through violence, fear, intimidation and the all time goodie of murder. Most mobsters could become violent and enraged by a single comment, by a feeling of betrayal, by someone caught being a rat, and especially by power plays. It was a world of ugly, lasting for decades and for many it was a new world of fascinating history.

What was happening to Dora and Cloud was not history. It was the present day dead and deadly serious.

The kidnappers were inept and bungled what they had been told to do. Their only instructions, "Keep them tied up and hidden in The Mob Museum until I tell you otherwise."

Who the leader was would become apparent soon enough, but the two men, were impetuous and impatient.

"What do you want from us?" Dora was hoping to get them to talk to her, to create a bond of some sort.

"Be quiet. You'll find out," Gordi answered. Kody was on the phone trying to reach their contact.

"Why won't you just talk to us, tell us what you want. Do you want money? We can get you plenty of money."

"Lady shut up, we'll let you know what we want soon enough."

Kody went over to his pal. "No answer. We better wait."

They paced and talked much too much about things they shouldn't have, tried making calls again, and slowly became more and more anxious. Not sure what to do next. Their contact was not there and not answering their phone calls.

All the time Cloud was twisting the ropes she had

been tied with, working to untie her hands. Dora noticed and sat silent, not wanting them to get near enough to see what Cloud was doing.

"Maybe we should look upstairs and see if anyone is waiting there for us. They're not going anywhere tied to those chairs."

As soon as they left the room Cloud moved quickly, finished untying herself, then Dora. "Let's get out of here." They raced out in the opposite direction from their kidnappers.

Meanwhile, it was Buzz and his band of characters that had found the car first and quickly alerted Dick who immediately informed the sheriff.

In some respects it was like a Marx Brothers Comedy. Buzz's motley crew running up and down the street shouting when the police arrived. "They're in there. There, in there. Hurry, hurry."

Sheriff Foster screamed, "Break the door down. Hold your guns. We don't want any shooting if possible." He called out for Dora and Cloud as they burst into The Mob Museum.

Dick and Zero shouted for them as they were running around the museum.

Dora and Cloud trying not to laugh since everyone was so proud of rescuing them, although they had managed to escape from the kidnappers on their own.

Dora and Cloud would later tell what went on before the cavalry arrived.

And still, no one was really sure who had arranged for the kidnapping, not even Kody or Gordi the fools who were taken out sobbing.

Chapter Forty-Four

Fools Errands

"They talked a lot when we were in the museum telling each other how with everything they knew they could get them a lot of money from Jane Kohl and Benjamin Rothstein.

Cloud looked at Dora, explaining what happened. "Go ahead. I was only along for the ride."

"Kody told his pal he listened to many of his father's conversations pretending he wasn't paying attention. Jane found out Benjamin Rothstein hired her own husband, Zachary, to kill her because she had those damning photos of him and she knew he cheated the syndicate."

Cloud would later talk about the syndicate, but this wasn't the time.

Dora continued, "He paid his son to threaten Shannon Flynn because she happened to walk past Jane showing him a couple of the photos. Shannon saw them and then walked away. Benjamin was so paranoid at this point he was making more and more stupid decisions. Shannon fought them which is why they decided to kill her. Gordi helped him get the icebox and take it with the body out to the desert or something like that. It was confusing from then on. I couldn't make sense of their nonsense."

"They admitted whoever hired them left money at The Black Tie for Kody and never said who it was and of course that person didn't show up at The Mob Museum. "Gordi, he was bragging about Rothstein hiring him to pretend he shot at him."

"Did he know why he wanted him to pretend he was being shot?"

"Something about the casino syndicate. You'll have to talk them.

"So Jane and Benjamin arranged for you to be kidnapped?" The sheriff was annoyed and relieved.

"I don't really think so."

♦ ♣ ♥ ♠

News Story: Caper at The Mob Museum

Murder and Mayhem took over the Las Vegas Mob Museum this past week when two women were kidnapped in front of the Smith Center for the Performing Arts and taken to the basement of the museum.

The story went on to describe the events according to the two abducted women. "It's as if Lucky Luciano, Bugsy Siegel and Al Capone came together with the Three Stooges. The kidnappers were running after us past photos of decades of mobster figures, images from famous gangster movies, from early to modern noir, and exhibits of crime and criminals."

The reporter asked the women, one a retired Manhattan judge, Dora Zimmerman, and the other Cloud, a Native American and senior investigator for the Bureau

M. Glenda Rosen

of Indian Affairs.

How did you manage to get away from them?
For the most part they were confused and unorganized. Once they got us into the basement, they told us to sit down and be quiet. When they went upstairs, Cloud managed to untie us both. She had her gun out of her handbag and we ran up some back stairs.
Did they try to catch up with you?
Yes, of course, when they came back downstairs and saw we were gone.
Then what happened?
We ran past the 'Wall of Infamy' and all I could think of is these idiots running after us would be mowed down by those mobsters if they were still alive.
Cloud, what about you and your gun?
"Had it in my pocket by now; meantime they ran right past us. We were hiding in a corner behind some mobster photos and they looked so ridiculous. One was tripping, looked like he was drunk or high, and the other one we could see was practically crying, and they were yelling at each other.

They finally realized we must be hiding nearby so as they turned to come back we went to the upper floors hiding again until we heard the police sirens, the front doors to the museum opening with the alarm blaring and shouts from the police, Dick and Zero.

The rest of the news story described the two men who kidnapped them and about others in the community under suspicion of murder, attempted murder and other assorted criminal acts.

The paper also went on to mention the Casino Syndicate stealing millions from Indian Casinos. "We've been told at this time there is no comment from the department handling that investigation."

Dora read the article aloud to the people gathered who had helped find her and Cloud. Buzz and his pals were enjoying the food and telling tall tales of their own adventures and misadventures over the years.

Dick and Zero, well what could they do about two such charming women.

Cloud looked over at Dora. They were sitting across from each other in the Zimms' condo smiling as she again patted her handbag.

The media would have plenty more stories as the drama unfolded. The story about the kidnapping had opened the door to further police investigations and to a web of deceit, secrets and lies that spanned dozens of years.

Chapter Forty-Five

The Photos

T he photos were one cause of his problems.

He had put on a dress, makeup and a blond wig.

Jane watched, fascinated.

Benjamin Rothstein had dressed himself to look like a woman.

They'd had sex a few hours earlier in his suite at The Black Tie. Now pretending to be asleep, Jane quietly took her phone off the nightstand while he was in the bathroom. At first shocked, stunned, yet wanting to laugh out loud, her gut instinct told her to remain still.

"Take photos," she told herself. "They could come in handy someday."

The following morning, she woke to Benjamin watching the national news, wearing sweatpants and a Black Tie t-shirt.

"Good, you're up. I ordered breakfast for you. I'm going to the gym to exercise."

"You mean you didn't have enough exercise last night?"

Laughing, Rothstein leaned over and gave her a kiss on the cheek and left the suite.

It was only sex for both of them. Over the past

couple years, without his knowing, Jane had taken photos a half dozen times of him dressed in women's clothing. He had no idea until the day she decided to blackmail him.

When she became aware of his wanting to eliminate her from the casino syndicate she played her hand and showed him a few of the many photos. Throwing them across the room, he first told her, "Destroy them. You have no right to expose my private life."   She laughed at him.

He then warned her, "Be careful, dear, I can make you disappear."

"True, Benjy, which is why I left a letter for my lawyer and another for each member of the casino syndicate to receive along with a packet of these photos in case anything happens to me...such as disappearing."

With Jane Kohl leaving his suite and his bed for the last time, Benjamin Rothstein knew he had a problem. He had been reckless around her and it was going to cost him dearly. Because now, someone else had mistakenly also seen the photos.

Benjy, devious and manipulative set up others to take the blame for the murder of Shannon Flynn. Unfortunately she had been in the wrong place at the wrong time, seen a couple of the photos and the cost was her life.

Acting stupid as though they were like old time mobsters they grabbed her when she left work at The Black Tie.

"If you tell anyone what you saw, he'll have you killed."

"Yeah, and he means business."

The two went back and forth like that for over ten

M. Glenda Rosen

minutes, when she kicked one of them and tried to run away. They told this story much later to the police when the foolish, ridiculous, criminal things they had done finally caught up with them.

"I grabbed her while he strangled her. She went limp and was lying by the back entrance of the hotel. We put her in my van parked there and drove away from the hotel."

"I had a connection to the university, got into the prop room and we took the icebox, and put it in the back of the van. It was late, no one was there. No one saw us."

"Yeah that's when we decided we should go out to the desert. It was a good idea."

The sheriff and one of his deputies sat listening amazed at the pride in their stupidity. "Then what?"

"When we got out of town, we picked a spot, there was no traffic late at night so we dragged the icebox out a ways, came back for the body and stuffed it inside."

"Yeah but you had the idea for the notes."

The dynamic duo of stupidity and incompetence were Gordi and Kody.

All this came to the light of day once they had been arrested for kidnapping Dora and Cloud. They were only pawns in the maneuverings of volatile people willing to destroy others for their own vanity.

When told all this no one was surprised at the details and stupidity of the whole story.

Chapter Forty-Six

Frankie Socks

In an overnight envelope to the Zimmermans in Las Vegas, with the return address, John Smith, Frankie Socks sent the damning letter along with photos of Benjamin Rothstein looking ridiculous he had found in Jane Kohl's Manhattan apartment.

"We need to get these to Foster." Dick passed the photos on to Dora. They were stunned at the photos of a man who acted so macho, who was a brute to his son and charged around The Black Tie Hotel and Casino bullying employees.

An hour after receiving them, sitting in his private office, Dick presented the overnight envelope to the sheriff, shrugging his shoulders, Dora silent. They knew what they had Frankie Socks do to get into Jane Kohl's apartment was not exactly kosher.

"How did you get these?"

"A friend," Dick said stoically.

"A friend? John Smith it says on the envelope. Really, John Smith? Who is this John Smith?" Foster asked, staring at the two of them.

"I think what matters Brady is what's in the envelope not who it's from."

"I think what matters is you two and your pals are interfering with a murder investigation."

Dora reached over to look at one of the photos. "Don't you dare touch them."

"Come on Brady, aren't you going to arrest her?"

"How about I arrest the two of you?"

"Why, Officer? We're innocent."

Glaring at Dick and Dora, the sheriff got up to leave, stopped and turned. Looking at Dick and being quite sarcastic he said, "When are you going to get rid of that growth on your face?"

Chapter Forty-Seven

Proof

"Send officers to arrest Benjamin Rothstein and Jane Kohl. Read them their Miranda Rights and put them in separate rooms," Foster told his deputy.

"What charges?"

"Conspiracy to commit murder and murder."

"Sheriff, they'll scream for their lawyers even before they get here."

"I don't give a damn. We have plenty of proof. The coroner and forensics are on their way here."

The coroner, Charlie Hughes, had worked with Foster for years. Once tall and lean, he now had a pot-belly, yellow teeth and a voice raspy from a cigar habit. Hughes was bent over from years of leaning over bodies brought to the morgue. There had been no end of joking about his last name.

"Where you hiding your millions, Hughes? Can you fix me up with some movie stars?" Over the years he ignored such comments.

Walking in with Hughes was the newest member of their forensic team. All two of them now. Short blond hair, dark blue eyes and slender, Faith Miller was in her late thirties and came with strong qualifications and a limp thanks to an abusive parent.

Sheriff Foster had the photos of Zachary Kohl on one end of the large conference table and photos of Shannon Flynn on the other.

Charlie began with Kohl's murder. "He clearly died of arsenic poison added to the flask."

"Any other evidence on the plane or with his belongings?" Foster turned to Faith.

"The crime scene at the airport was tight. We went through the entire first class section and then back to coach, didn't find anything else. We have the housekeeper's fingerprints on the flasks screw cap. But…"

"But what?"

"I noticed a smell on Kohl's briefcase."

Sheriff Foster, leaned back, interested. "And?"

"It's an expensive perfume sold in high end department stores."

"Possibly the kind someone like Jane Kohl would use?"

"Absolutely. It could prove she handled the brief case before he left."

Turner reminded the sheriff, "There is also the key Dora Zimmerman found."

Glaring, Foster stood up to get coffee set up on a small corner table, "Don't remind me. Maybe a few days in holding would do them good."

Hughes laughed out loud. He'd heard these comments about Dick and Dora from Foster many times. "Okay, Chief, moving on to Shannon Flynn's murder. It's gruesome and more sloppy."

Foster picked up the photos taken of her at the morgue. "This is an awful thing to do to anyone. Any evidence you found might be helpful?"

"She was strangled before being stuffed into the icebox. There's fingerprints and DNA on her neck, the icebox and the notes. No she wasn't sexually assaulted. I brought you photos showing print matches we found in the system. Oh, also, there were a few casino chips found in one of her pockets. They're from The Black Tie Casino."

"Sheriff, you have plenty to take this to the district attorney to pursue an indictment for her murder. Fingerprints and DNA match those of Kody Rothstein and Gordi Erickson."

After Hughes and Faith left, the sheriff was thinking about the murders, the victims, and the suspects, but something was bothering him. All the pieces of this puzzle didn't fit right, not yet as far as he was concerned.

"My gut is telling me something and someone more sinister is involved."

Chapter Forty-Eight

Missing

The officers sent to pick up Benjamin and Jane made an urgent call. "Sheriff, they're both missing."

Foster was less than thrilled at this turn of events, shouting, "Did you try his suite, or the casino and restaurants? Also the garage, see if his car is there."

"Yes sir, checked everywhere and his car is there. We tried contacting his security manager, Glenn Erickson, but he wasn't answering his phone."

"And Jane Kohl?"

"She checked out of her hotel this morning. Doorman said she got into a taxi. Heard her say 'star.'"

"Get over to The Star. Turner and I are on our way."

Turner called Dick as Foster drove with siren blaring. "You and Dora are in danger. The sheriff and I are on our way to see you now. Seems Jane Kohl may be on her way to harm you."

"The lady is crazed and has already made her intentions to murder us known. Dora and I were about to call you."

"Tell the sheriff she was banging on our door and when we refused to let her in she shot several rounds into the door. We're fine. Zero came up the back stairs, thought maybe he could charm her into calming down. When she saw him she turned and ran, screaming obscenities as she got into the elevator."

"Stay inside."

"Gladly."

Dick opened the door to the police. Curious neighbors were sneaking peeks through partially opened doors. Buzz and Zero had managed to get inside with them when Kohl ran off,

"This is quite a party." Dick acted much more lighthearted than he felt.

"Did you hear her say where she might be going?" Sheriff Foster was not in any mood for Dick's frivolity.

Dora, wearing pale yellow satin pajamas with a matching robe, stood up, went over to the windows showing a view of the city. "If I was a betting woman, I would say she's headed for New York."

Zero nodded. "As a betting man I agree."

Everyone thought it best not to make any comment to a man who was wearing red sweatpants and a black t-shirt with orange lettering, "Don't tell me what to do."

One of the deputies put out an "armed and dangerous" call for Jane Kohl and notified security at McCarran airport as Foster told everyone, "She's not the only one who might have a grudge against you. You've annoyed quite a few people. Benjamin Rothstein is missing and we have a warrant out for his arrest."

"For murder?" Dora asked moving next to Dick while Buzz and Zero were whispering to each other.

"Yes."

"You have proof?" asked Dick

"His son and his pal Gordi provided us with plenty of it."

"He'll say they're lying."

"Give us some credit for knowing how to do our job."

Dora excused herself to get dressed. Dick excused himself to get a scotch and water. "Never too early to drink when someone has tried to kill you."

Sheriff Foster, looking at the bullet marks on the front of their door shook his head and rolled his eyes hoping this threat would stop these people from interfering further. Although he doubted it.

"Turner, get Faith Miller over here to check for fingerprints and type of gun used." As he was about to leave the sheriff's cell phone rang. "Jane Kohl's at the airport."

"Lock your door. We still can't find Rothstein."

"You bet." Dick nodded in a way far from assuring Sheriff Foster.

"And wait here for Faith Miller from forensics."

He left without waiting for a response. Once again sirens blared through the busy Vegas streets, whisking him to the airport, to Jane Kohl, to a dangerous situation where crowds of people would be milling around the terminal.

McCarran airport had slots throughout the terminal. It was a casino unto itself and players oblivious to anything else would be easy targets.

"I have a feeling this is going to get much worse before it's over," Sheriff Foster said to Deputy Turner as they pulled in front of the airport entrance. Several police cars behind them did the same.

Unfortunately so did Benjamin Rothstein. He had followed Jane to The Star and after she ran out and got into another taxi he followed her to the airport using Glenn Erickson's car.

Much later when all this had ended with minimal damage it would be easy to feel as if it was a Marx Brothers and Three Stooges comedy act all in one. The behavior of so many was so irrational it bordered on lunacy.

Rothstein called Glenn Erickson to his suite before 6AM even though he had quit, begging him for one last favor. "Give me your keys. I need to use your car."

Glenn seeing the craziness in his eyes made the mistake of shaking his head no and turned to leave. Rothstein hit him over the head with the butt of a weapon he planned to use on Jane, then on Dick and Dora, "her pals."

Before Erickson arrived Benjamin removed from a locked cabinet, a Remington Model 870 shotgun, popular with mobsters and the law during the 1950's.

According to the National Crime Syndicate website it was "a lethal and powerful weapon, one of the top five used by the Mob."

He had kept the weapon once used by his father. Periodically he would take it out, and polish it, rubbing it as if it was an old lover, making sure it was always loaded.

Rothstein had gone way beyond over the edge.

Chapter Forty-Nine

Gun Shots

Dora knew she couldn't stop him.

As soon as the sheriff left, Dick went into high gear. "Zero, stay here with Dora in case Rothstein heads this way."

"Hey, I can take care of myself, big boy," Dora said, indignant at the thought she might need watching.

"Yes dear, you can, but a little help from our friends is a good idea. Plus the forensics lady is on her way. Best she talk to you."

"Yeah, fine. Cloud is on her way. She insisted on being here with us."

Dick tugged at Buzz. "Get the car. I want to go to the airport."

Once in the car, he said, "Dick, why are we doing this?"

"We've known each other for years. Maybe I can stop him from doing something even more stupid." He was referring to Rothstein.

"Doesn't mean anything once someone gets this out of control."

Buzz sped to the airport on the side streets he knew so well.

By the time they got to the airport chaos had broken out. Police were rushing inside, travelers scrambling to get away from the terminal, an ambulance nearing and news on the police scanner. "One person shot, gunman has a hostage."

Suddenly they saw Rothstein dragging a young girl out of the terminal. She was sobbing as he waved the shotgun, pulled a driver out of a car, threw him and the girl on the ground then drove out of the airport into city traffic.

"Follow him." Dick turned up the scanner.

"I can't believe he got away from the police, must be a dozen here."

"Buzz, quiet, listen."

"Airport gunman, Benjamin Rothstein, owner of The Black Tie Hotel and Casino is armed and dangerous. Do not approach. Repeat. Do not approach. One woman shot as she walked out of the ladies room heading toward security. He's in a stolen car."

The make and model of the car and the license number were given over the scanner.

Driving behind the stolen car onto the freeway, Dick experienced something close to panic realizing where Rothstein seemed to be headed. "I have to tell the sheriff we're behind him."

"Right, and if Rothstein doesn't kill us he will."

"Chance we have to take, he's headed to The Star."

Luckily, Turner answered.

"Buzz and I are behind Rothstein. He's headed to my place."

"What are you doing behind him?"

"Happened to be at the airport and saw him leaving."

"You're following him?"

Hearing Turner, Foster bellowed, "Damn it, stay away from him. He shot Jane Kohl at the airport. I'll get more officers to The Star. Call your wife and warn her."

"Yes, sir."

"Don't give me that Yes Sir B.S."

"No sir, I mean, oh what the hell, Sheriff. Bye."

Click.

Calling Dora next, he said, "Benjamin has a loaded shotgun and is on his way to The Star. He shot Jane at the airport."

"Is she dead?" Dora slowly sat down next to Cloud. She and Faith had both arrived at the same time a few minutes earlier.

"Who is dead?" mouthed Cloud.

"Jane."

Dick shouted, "Dora who are you talking to?"

"Cloud."

"Are police still outside our condo door?"

"Yes. You didn't answer me. Is Jane dead?"

"Don't know. More police are on the way. Don't do anything foolish, he's panicked and clearly volatile. I'll be there soon. One thing I do know is I don't want you dead."

"Yes, dear."

Chapter Fifty

Fight or Flight

Glenn Erickson came to in Rothstein's hotel suite with a sore head and his car keys missing. He immediately notified the police only to discover his now former boss had already shot Jane Kohl and was on the run.

"He's headed to Dick and Dora Zimmerman's. It would be wise to alert your Black Tie security people. He's carrying a shotgun and willing to use it." Turner was shouting over the sound of the sirens.

"Okay, but a memorial service is planned for Shannon Flynn at five p.m. in The Tuxedo Café. I have no way to reach everyone to cancel it."

"We'll send over a few officers. Get everyone from Black Tie Security there for the rest of the day and if he shows up call us immediately."

"Of course." Glenn went to put an ice pack on his head as he made several calls, one to Krupe, Shannon's friend who helped plan the memorial. Explaining the situation, he told him, "Come early. Just in case."

"I'll be there by three."

Next Erickson arranged to have everyone from The Black Tie security detail at the café by one. "Just in case," he told them.

They would be ready.

They had no idea what to expect and it turned out no one could have predicted the events about to occur involving the owner of The Black Tie Hotel and Casino.

Glenn knew one thing for certain, you couldn't reason with the man, he had tried many times over the years. Now Dick was going to make the same worthless effort.

Dick parked a couple car lengths behind Benjamin at The Star, waited for him to get out of the stolen car and then attempted to reason with him.

"I know Jane tried to hurt you. You have every right to be upset."

Standing behind Dick, Buzz wisecracked in a whisper, "Yeah, he looks adorable in those women's clothes."

"Quiet."

"Sorry, Boss." Dick knew Buzz wasn't at all sorry.

Chances were some of the photos of Benjamin dressed as a woman would appear in newspapers, even on Facebook. The world had changed in a very short time. Others could see your foibles or in this case, someone's idea of fashion.

"Come on Benjamin, there's police here, more on the way. I don't want to see you get hurt or worse."

"Give me a break, you don't care about me. You only want to be sure your precious wife and friends aren't at the other end of my shotgun. I assure you, pal, I know how to use it."

Attempting another tactic to calm him down, Dick said, "Benjamin, you're actually a hero finding Jane. She's responsible for having her husband killed."

"Yeah, you're right. I am a hero."

Buzz, once again with a quiet wisecrack, "He

should be rewarded with twenty years to life."

Dick gave Buzz a dirty look and turned to see Benjamin heading toward The Star, running through its desert-like landscaping, briefly stopping to shout and wave his gun like he was Al Capone.

"You think I don't know a con when I hear one? My old man could have taken all of you out with this gun. He would have enjoyed it. Maybe I will too."

The sheriff was now next to Dick and talk about dirty looks. "What's he been saying?"

"Wants to kill me."

"It would save me the job."

"Thanks, love you too. I've been trying to reason with him. Told me he knows how to use the gun."

"He does. Shot Jane She probably won't make it."

Later Dick would tell Dora, "You had to see it to believe it. It could only happen in the movies...yet here it was...prancing out of the back entrance of The Star was Dame Isabella. Somehow she managed to get past the police."

"Damn it, Turner, find out what's going on in there." The sheriff urged her to get back inside.

"What's going on? I go for a walk."

"Get back inside, now."

"I will not. I wait for my Zero. He might come for me. I leave him a message I be here."

Dame Isabella did have a killer outfit on. Long, bright red dress, red shoes, hair and makeup done.

"Dressed to kill comes to mind, Boss," commented Buzz.

Sheriff Foster glared at both of them.

Her showing up distracted everyone long enough for Benjamin to run away from The Star, down several blocks and over to a main street where he hailed a taxi, the shotgun wrapped in his jacket.

Several police officers followed him on foot, others in police cars.

Dick and Buzz ran upstairs, the sheriff coming after them.

"Have you lost your mind?"

"No, Sheriff, no, I, well I. I don't think so, not really." Dick was unusually flustered. Mostly he was relieved Benjamin had not gotten into The Star.

"He could have killed you and your traveling companion here."

"Sir, I am only his driver. To quote an old TV character, 'I know nothing.'"

Turner was now on his cell phone frantic and shouting, "Sheriff, he circled back to The Star, ran into the back entrance and grabbed the lady dressed in red before we could get her inside."

"Will you listen to me for a change?" Foster was in no mood for their wisecracks. "Benjamin is clearly headed to your condo."

"My condo is three floors down from here," Zero said.

"Good, go there, now."

Escorted by two police officers everyone now in the Zimms' condo followed them down to Zero's. Unlike the Zimmermans', it faced away from the view of the city lights and out to miles of desert.

"Well isn't this fun, a marching party," Buzz whispered to Zero walking down the steps.

"I hope I win a prize for best dressed," joked Zero.

Zero's clothing tastes went from bizarre to outrageous. Although he seemed a bit more subdued around

Cloud.

Speaking of high fashion, Dame Isabella was still a problem for the police...and Zero.

Chapter Fifty-One

Now What?

Benjamin grabbed Dame Isabella before the police could reach her, pulling her inside the condo building.

"You let me go. My Zero hurt you."

"Be quiet. I gotta think."

The front entrance of the condo building was in lock down with armed officers while more were inside checking common areas and hallways. Benjamin hearing them realized he needed a way out.

"Old lady, where is the kitchen?"

Silence.

Picking up her tiny frame, his hands around her throat, he spit into her face, "Show me where the kitchen is or I'll strangle you. I swear I will."

Frightened, she replied, "End of hall go left, you see it from there."

She winced as he pushed her down on a seat next to the elevator.

Benjamin was too frantic to notice her reach over and push the elevator button.

Limping in pain she got on and went to Zero's condo when she saw the police standing there.

"Tell my Zero, let me in. Help, I'm hurt. Big fat man threatened and pushed me."

They let her in and Zero sat her on his sofa. Dora got an ice pack for her swelling ankle.

Dick asked where Benjamin was. "He go to kitchen."

Cloud asked Dame Isabella if she wanted something to drink. The Dame gave her a dirty look and told her, "Go away, Zero mine."

"Yes, dear, of course he is."

Dick called the sheriff. "Rothstein is headed to the kitchen."

"Must be an exit there."

"Need some help?"

"Yeah, staying out of our way."

Dora put her arm around Dick. "I'm glad Dame Isabella doesn't want you sweetheart." Zero raised his eyebrows and shook his head.

Dick's cell phone rang silencing everyone. Emotions ranged from fear to concern. Dora still standing next to him, he showed her it was Rothstein. Since an officer remained in the condo with them, Dick clearly didn't want him to know who it was.

"Sorry, I have to cancel our dinner plans. We are otherwise occupied."

"What the hell you talking about?" Rothstein screamed.

"Wondering what it is you want?"

"I want to kill your sorry life."

"Well I'm not available. Perhaps we could negotiate some other option."

"Yeah, and perhaps I might shoot the old lady."

"Sorry it's also no longer an option. She's here with

us."

"What?"

"Perhaps now we can meet?"

Benjamin slid down onto the floor of the kitchen the gun lying next to him figuring maybe he could take Dick as a hostage.

"I'll come talk to you."

Moving the gun onto his lap, Rothstein said, "Fine."

Slipping the phone in his pocket, Dick pulled Zero toward him. "Come with me. The rest of you stay here."

"I will not let you go without me," shouted Dora.

"Officer, hold this woman, the sheriff wants to see me and this nice man."

Before the officer had a chance to check with the sheriff, Dick and Zero were out the door and headed downstairs while the officer held on to Dora who was furious, and shouting. "Dick Zimmerman if you get killed, I swear I'll kill you."

Chapter Fifty-Two

His Father's Son

B enjamin was aware of an eerie silence. The hallways were empty, lights dim and the only sounds he heard were wind chimes ringing outdoors, the desert winds were announcing their presence. The police had the condo building on lockdown, residents warned to stay inside their homes. Not all listened.

Entering the kitchen, his shadow was on the wall as he passed shiny counters, appliances and hanging cookware. Searching desperately for an exit, he found himself in the dining area. Going back into the kitchen he opened another door leading to a food storage locker. Finally he found the exit where garbage was taken out, the police were stationed at the end of the long alleyway.

Slamming the exit door shut, panicked and cornered, Benjamin Rothstein figured he would take Dick as a hostage. His planning didn't go much further.

Zero and Dick took the stairs, two at a time Getting to the first floor, Dick took his cell phone out of his jacket pocket, "Sheriff, just listen, you can yell later. Rothstein says he wants to talk to me. Zero and I are on the first floor not far from the kitchen. Tell me what to say to him."

"Don't get any closer, his shotgun can blow you

away if he gets trigger happy. Understand?"

"Yes, tell me what to say, maybe I can get him to surrender himself peacefully."

"Ask him if he's hurt? Make him feel like you're concerned about him."

"Then what?"

Suddenly they heard shots coming from the kitchen.

"Find out what's happening. I'll stay on the line."

"Benjamin, it's Dick. Are you hurt? Do you need help?"

"How do the police know where I am?"

"The old lady you dragged into the building, you asked her how to get to the kitchen?"

"I should have shot her."

"Benjamin, she's a harmless old woman. You should know Jane and Kody told the sheriff they committed the murders."

"Kid was always trouble."

"Give yourself up. You can explain how you were protecting yourself from Jane's threats."

"Damn straight. My father would be proud of me. He taught me how to take care of anyone who betrays me."

"You were lucky."

"Yeah. Sure I was, still am."

"Dick, can you get me out of here so the cops don't shoot me?"

The sheriff listening to the conversation asked Dick, "Where is he?"

Zero managed to get to the kitchen entrance and take a quick look. "He's standing in a corner by the door. Could be a food pantry or freezer. The shotgun is on the counter next to him."

"Keep him talking, get him tired."

"Where do you want to go Benjamin?"

"My suite at The Black Tie."

"Police are already there."

"Maybe where Deidre lives. She has a home on the other side of town."

"How about I call her and see if she'll be okay with you coming there."

"Never mind. Bitch will say no."

Dick kept talking to the man who truly had no way out. Zero kept watch. It took more than two hours until Benjamin who had been up and down, pacing and shouting, slid down exhausted.

"Sheriff, he's on the floor by the pantry door. When you come in the kitchen exit it's off to your immediate right."

It happened so quickly Rothstein had no chance to stand up or reach for his gun. Hostile and trying to get away, his clothes were disheveled from being on the floor, his face red and clammy. As he was handcuffed and read his rights, he kept shouting, "Give me my gun, damn it. It's mine." They took the Mob rifle that had killed far too many people in years past.

Word spread to the memorial at The Tuxedo Café and everyone there applauded.

There was no love lost for the Rothstein's.

For some reason Dick felt some pieces were still missing.

"You two, be at the police station at nine tomorrow morning. I want you there when we talk to him. Consider yourselves lucky to be alive."

"I don't think he would have shot us."

"I'm referring to me." The sheriff turned and headed to the police station.

Nodding yes, knowing better than to say another word, Dick and Zero went to face Dora and Cloud.

"Was he really cornered?" asked Dora.

Zero, not one to let a cliché or bet pass him by, commented, "You bet he was."

Chapter Fifty-Three

Life Can Be Murder At Times

While the drama took place downstairs in the condo kitchen the three women alone in Zero's home discussed justice, truth and survival. Faith forced to remain behind in the safety of the condo found herself in the company of two exceptional women.

This was no ordinary day and no ordinary group of women.

Buzz and a police officer took a fussy Dame Isabella to her own condo, several doors away from Zero. The sheriff gave his okay with Benjamin locked down in the kitchen.

"Take her home and both of you stay with her until it's safe to call for an ambulance to take her to the hospital."

Pain and the frightening incident had calmed her quest for love, for now.

"What's most important to each of you?" Cloud asked. "We might as well talk about something interesting while we wait."

Dora replied, "Justice, especially for children and the elderly."

Faith, surprised she had the courage, said, "Survival."

Cloud replied, "Mine is truth."

"As a lawyer, then a judge, my life, both mine and Dick's, have been about helping bring justice to where there are injustices. There are good people who deserve a system doing its best to ensure they get it, and see the bad guys pay for their injustices."

"Still there are those who commit murder believing they can get away with it," Faith said softly.

Staring at Faith, hoping she would tell her survival story, Dora replied, "At times they do. The good guys don't always win. It's not a perfect system. It is, however, the best I know of after being a part of it for over forty years."

Turning to Cloud, Faith giving her a warm smile, "So, truth?"

Dora knew it was a complicated issue for Cloud. One she would have to face with Zero, soon.

Cloud rubbed her hands as she spoke. "In the work I've chosen to do, there are times it's been necessary for me to hold back on certain truths. It's odd thinking about it because the essence of my work is finding the truth and exposing those who attempt to exploit and harm my culture."

"Does that mean you would lie for what you might consider the greater good?" Faith asked, intrigued.

"It depends on the needs of a situation. Faith, similar to justice, there are times it might require misleading a bad person in order to get them to admit their guilt, or even give up the name of someone they know who committed a crime or murder."

"Unfortunately there are times when getting to the truth and justice requires a bit of wiggle room." Dora long held this point of view with great conviction.

Cloud realized she was rubbing her hands. "Silly habit from childhood."

The Las Vegas sky had turned dark threatening rain, a city stirring and restless.

"A murderer ran into the airport, shot a woman, likely dead, the gunman on the loose," local television stations stated over and over as they are known to do.

The police, with help from Dick and Zero had been desperately playing out Benjamin's next act floors below the women's conversation.

Faith stood staring out the window. "He tried to rape me. He wanted to murder me."

Dora and Cloud sensed to not say a word so she would continue.

"The first time was when I was twelve. My father tried to rape me. I shoved him hard and was able to get away because he was drunk. I went to live with my mother's younger sister. She lived in a different Los Angeles neighborhood, far enough away for me to feel safe. I visited my mother only when I knew he wouldn't be home. He was often drunk and abusive to my mother and no matter how many times I begged her to leave him she wouldn't, said she couldn't. I never understood, I still don't"

"Did he try to see you?" Dora asked quietly

"No. He knew my aunt would call the police. She had an order of protection forbidding him to be anywhere near her house or me. She was tough but kind to me. She taught me the importance of education and believing in oneself. She gave me love and saved my life. I wish she could have done the same for my mother."

"What happened to your leg?" Cloud asked softly.

Faith sat down, touching her damaged leg. "I went to visit my mother when he wasn't supposed to be there. He came home early screaming. Suspected I was visiting her when he wasn't home. He pushed me down, said now he would get a piece of me and tried to rape me again. My mother hit him on the head, I think with a cooking pot. I ran to my aunt's, she gave me money and said I should take a bus to Las Vegas. She had a good friend there, wrote down her name and phone number and told me she would send my things to me after I let her know I was there."

"But you didn't get to leave?" Cloud asked.

"No. He followed me to my aunt's, saw me get in a taxi and when I got out tried to pull me into his truck, cursing and calling me all sorts of disgusting names. His head was bleeding from where he had been hit. I punched him where I saw he was hurt and while he howled in pain, I ran but he started the truck intentionally running me over crushing my left leg."

"Faith, how horrible." Dora went over and hugged the young woman. Cloud was in tears.

"Even worse he went home took a gun he had in his glove compartment and killed my mother. The police who had his license plate from some people who witnessed what he did to me caught him. He's in jail for life, no chance of parole. When I was well my aunt helped me to go to college. I got a partial scholarship and majored in Criminal Justice and Forensic Sciences. I worked in L.A. a few years and when I saw the listing for this job in Las Vegas I felt like it was a calling for a new beginning. I have no brothers or sisters, my aunt passed away a couple years ago, so, I decided it was another road to survival."

"Has your father tried to contact you?" Dora asked

still next to her.

"Oh yes, writes me, says he's a changed man and to forgive him. I burn his letters."

"Good," Cloud commented.

Dora nodded her head in agreement.

The sound of sirens outside, the knock on Zero's door and Dick shouting open up was almost perfect timing. Justice, trust and survival were ready to take their place along with relief.

Zero and Dick, tired and relieved, explained, "He's been arrested but not without a fight. Dora we have to be at the station at nine tomorrow morning. I'll explain why in a bit. How about a drink? After all we've been busy slaying dragons for you lovely ladies."

Dora went over and hugged Dick.

"Yes of course you have, dear."

The three women smiled. They had slayed a few of dragons of their own the past few hours. Metaphorically speaking of course.

"Zero, we need to talk." Cloud gave him a hug.

"First a toast." Dick plopped down next to Dora and sighed. "To Jane Kohl and Benjamin Rothstein who did not manage to murder us this day."

Chapter Fifty-Four

Ultimate Betrayal

"It was my son."

Sitting with handcuffs on in a police station interrogation room, Kody's father blamed him for everything.

"What about Jane Kohl? Benjamin you shot her at the airport."

Foster had a psychologist who worked special cases for the police department observe Rothstein being questioned. As furious as the sheriff was with Dick he realized it could be valuable for him to listen to the interrogation. "Maybe you'll recall something Rothstein said when he was cornered in the condo kitchen."

The sheriff had begrudgingly agreed. "Yeah. Dora should come too. Her years as a judge might prove helpful. I don't want any of your cute remarks during the interrogation."

"Promise." Dick holding up his hand like a boy scout asked, "Where's his attorney?"

"Out of town. He's screaming for him, nothing we can do about it."

The sheriff continued to accuse Benjamin of murder and attempted murder.

"I did not kill anyone."

"There were more than half a dozen witnesses who saw you shoot her at the airport."

"They're all liars, want money from me. I'm a rich man you know. They want my money."

Sitting back with his arrogant, smug attitude, Benjamin refused to acknowledge blame for his actions.

"Why did you have Shannon Flynn killed?"

"What? Who is she?"

"She was an employee of The Black Tie until you arranged for your son to take care of her."

"Why are you blaming me for what my son has done?"

Nodding yes, his deputy started the tape recorder. "Kody, here's five hundred bucks, I need you to threaten a woman who works at The Black Tie, Shannon Flynn. Take Gordi with you to scare her. She could cause big problems for me."

"Okay, I knew her. I thought she was going to blackmail me or try to embarrass me so I asked him to threaten her, nothing more."

"Why would she want to do that?"

"Damn it, Sheriff, she saw some compromising photos of me."

"You mean like the ones Jane had?"

"Yeah, so what. And I didn't order her to be killed."

The deputy played another tape. "My father told me if Shannon Flynn gave us any trouble, we should kill her and get rid of the body as far out of town as possible."

Benjamin appeared shocked and went to stand up. The sheriff forcefully pushed him back down. "He's lying. I know he is. You know he is."

"We don't really know he's lying. You listened to what he said on the tape."

"Bring him here. I'll ask the little S.O.B. He won't lie to my face."

After more than three hours of interrogation with constant denials from Rothstein, the psychologist commented to Dick and Dora, "He's got a good case for pleading insanity."

Sheriff Foster finally had had enough. "Put him back in a cell."

For Benjamin Rothstein, a moment of realty set in and he shouted, "Where the hell is my attorney?"

Dora whispered to her husband, "Something isn't right."

Chapter Fifty-Five

The Casino Conspiracy

"They organized a gaming racket draining millions from Indian casinos. They were emboldened by their success with one casino so they created a casino syndicate whose primary objective was to scheme, steal and embezzle casino monies from other Indian casinos."

"Are members of the syndicate all from Las Vegas?" Dick asked.

Zero had sat quiet while Cloud had explained who she was and her role as a senior investigator for the Bureau of Indian Affairs. Dick was curious.

"Yes. Four men, part owners of casinos here in Las Vegas plus Benjamin Rothstein and Jane Kohl. A couple also became investors in The Black Tie the last couple years. Benjamin was embezzling money from his own casino and needed an infusion of capital to keep it running."

"Cloud is this the reason you wanted to come to Las Vegas?" Everyone in the room looked at Zero.

"Originally, yes. It's changed because of you and I hope you believe me and forgive me."

"Zero, let Cloud tell us what else she's found out." Dora knew he was feeling bad but her longtime friend was also generous and understanding. He had to be with all life had thrown had him.

Cloud wore light beige cotton slacks, a soft white shirt and sandals. Zero looked at her while she continued. "I'm sure you know casinos on Indian land are owned partly by the tribe whose land it's on and partly by investors. And for many tribal communities it helped improve their lives substantially."

"Isn't there some controversy about the gaming industry and tribal nations?" questioned Dick.

"True. Some improved education, services, better roads and led to prosperous opportunities. Unfortunately many did not have this type of success. All kind of scams and schemes began to infiltrate the gaming world."

"Aren't there laws to stop and protect this from happening?" Zero had finally spoken up.

An encouraging sign, thought Cloud.

"There's the Indian Gaming Working Group created by the FBI and Native Indian Gaming Commission. Their work is to hopefully eliminate violations, identify criminal activities and assist in these investigations. Keep in mind gaming for the Native American Tribes is a billion-dollar industry."

"What's happening now to the people involved in the casino syndicate you've been investigating?" asked Dora, always concerned about justice.

"They've been notified they're officially under investigation for criminal wrong doing and their license to be a part of any Indian casino or gaming operation has been suspended. These are federal offenses and they'll pay heavy fines and probably go to jail."

"How did you get evidence on what they were

doing? As a lawyer, I can't help wondering how you managed to gather this evidence."

"Dick, we had a mole in the syndicate. I was his voice to and from the FBI, the gaming commission and other government agencies involved. It's obviously complicated."

"Were you ever in any danger?" Zero as the saying goes, was wearing his heart on his sleeve.

Cloud went over to Zero who was listening to every word as he leaned against the bar in the living room and took his hand. "Not really. I wanted to tell you but couldn't take a chance of jeopardizing something so many people worked on for the past several years. Forgive me. I never expected this when we first met online."

"Expected what?" Zero looked at her.

Dick and Dora sat quietly, not sure what was about to happen. They were worried and hopeful for a man they dearly cared about.

"To fall in love with you."

Chapter Fifty-Six

Something Isn't Right

D ick was tired, heading to bed, planning to read more about those who helped build America's legal and political system. Their behaviors and maneuverings fascinated him.

Dora wasn't at all tired, more like wired thinking about the murders, people involved in them and trusting her instincts. They had usually served her well.

"Something isn't right."

"Please, tell me you don't want me to sit with you and discuss what that might be."

"Okay, I won't tell you." There it was, her charming sarcasm he had grown to love, not so much.

Dick knew better, made an about face and joined her on the sofa, the blinds closed only flashes of light from neon signs outside fighting their way inside.

"You got me here, love, so, I repeat. What's not right?"

"Kody's story about Benjamin doesn't make any sense. And something about when Cloud and I were kidnapped has been bothering me."

"Such as?" Now alert and listening, he too trusted his wife's instincts. Throughout their marriage, their professions and especially their love for each other, he knew she had a tough inner core, tougher than his own. He quite admired her strengths. Not to mention the rest of her.

"Someone is pulling the strings."

"I assume you have a theory?"

"I do."

"How far back does this go?"

"To big money."

Dick was wide-awake.

"What evidence do you have to support this?" The lawyer was cross-examining.

Dora was prepared. Enclosed in an envelope sitting on the coffee table were articles from their friend and New York newspaper reporter Carson Gladstone. He was also a poker buddy of Dick's when in New York. He lost most of the time and usually paid his debt by doing favors for them. They knew the truth was he would have done them no matter what.

"Where did you get these?"

"From Carson." Dora sensed Dick's interest growing.

"I thought there might be articles to prove my little theory. He emailed them and I printed these few out, there's more."

"Not such a little theory, my dear."

"True." Dora sat with her feet curled up under her on their sofa. "Rather shocking, don't you think?"

"In a way it does explain some unusual happenings. Couple more things I'd like to know before we tell anyone else. " Dick got up to call Frankie Socks in Manhattan.

"Frankie, I need you to check out something for

me."

Eight hours later, Dick and Dora called the sheriff, told him what they had discovered and suggested, "How about if we get everyone connected to the murders, the mysteries, the crimes, anything you want and get them together in one place and soon."

"Hate to admit it but I was reviewing the cases and something didn't seem right to me either."

"I'll call Glenn Erickson. I'm sure he'll be willing to help us arrange a private party at The Tuxedo Café, especially since his brother is implicated in this mess."

"Tomorrow at five o'clock. I'll bring those in jail, along with police protection. You get the others there. I'll have Deputy Turner and some officers at the entrance of the café to check everyone for weapons. We've had enough shootouts with these characters."

As soon as Dick hung up he and Dora split the list of who was to be called. "Dora, I'll take care of Buzz and Zero, and I'll tell Glenn to have the musician Krupe there too."

"Fine, I'll get the ladies, darling, Cloud, Deidre and Faith. What about Dame Isabella?"

"Maybe, let's think about it for now."

When Frankie Socks had called them back, he told Dick, "It is exactly who and what you and Dora thought."

An actual thunderstorm was pounding the dark night. Many hid out in casinos gambling, others couldn't ignore its warning signs.

Chapter Fifty-Seven

Private Party

It was one of those special parities when everyone invited showed up. "Hard to turn down." Zero, standing next to Buzz, watched officers at the entrance check everyone for weapons.

"This should be fun. Leave it to Dick and Dora to plan this lovely soiree."

Dick had the chairs from the dining room tables arranged in a circle, a large square coffee table brought from one of the suites was in the middle, its use not yet defined.

A little before five o'clock, Sheriff Foster arrived with Benjamin, Kody and Gordi in handcuffs, each with a police officer escorting them. They had most definitely arrived in different police cars. If looks could kill they would all be passed out dead on the café floor.

Benjamin shouted as he walked in the room. "Take these damn handcuffs off me. I'm not a common criminal and this is my hotel."

Thus began the comment and at times comedy portion of the evening with Zero sitting between Dora and Cloud, commenting, "Maybe an uncommon criminal."

Dick orchestrating the private party as other so-called guests arrived had told Buzz to watch for anyone making sudden moves toward Dora or Cloud. Faith was next to the sheriff, folder in hand, she was there representing the coroner's office. Deputy Turner appeared to be on roving guard duty along with several other of Las Vegas' finest. "Be prepared for trouble," Foster told them at the station.

Soon, everyone was seated. Benjamin still complaining, the sheriff telling him, "Shut up." Kody sat quiet and scared, hands shaking, Gordi with tears, glancing frequently toward his brother.

Glenn explained to Dick and the sheriff, "Shannon's friend who worked at the Black Tie left Vegas after she got a call that told her to leave town or what happened to Shannon would happen to her."

"Did she say if it was a man or woman's voice?" Foster asked curious.

"Said she couldn't tell."

The party room was filling up.

Deidre arrived, dressed for something fancier than this event. She was rude and irritated. "You've interrupted my plans for the evening so I could sit here with this group of losers."

An officer almost dragged her to a chair next to Glenn. She continued ranting when Benjamin practically hissed, "You're the loser, sweetheart. No more money from the casino for you. Feds are closing it down." Clearly stunned, she demanded, "I need to leave immediately."

Dick calmly responded, "No one is leaving, not until the party is over."

"Do you know where he's going with this happy gathering?" Cloud leaned over Zero to ask Dora.

"Watch the wizard lawyer at work," Dora commented

Zero smiled, "Our Dick's a wizard, sweetheart, because you're his genius muse."

Dame Isabella, ultimately invited, came with her ankle wrapped, walking with a cane and was between Buzz and Krupe. She was intentionally seated away from Zero. Deidre was seated on the other side of Krupe. Two men who hardly anyone knew were also there seated near the three men under arrest whose handcuffs were taken off once everyone was seated.

"Delighted you could all attend. Please know, complaining, shouting, screaming or any other type of fussing will only delay this evening. Dick is in charge for now and Faith, the Las Vegas Police Department forensics expert will provide evidence when required." Sheriff Foster turned to Dick with a nod and went to stand behind the circle of people.

"Cooperate and we'll get this over with quickly and hopefully without anyone having to be dragged out of here and taken to police headquarters by one of the sheriff's men here."

The Tuxedo Café was usually full of gamblers taking a break or getting ready to start playing at their games of chance. At night lights were dimmed and tables were set with cream color tablecloths and matching napkins. Servers bustled and hustled from table to table. This night those tables were empty, there was another form of gambling taking place.

"We realize it's a gamble to bring everyone involved together, however, we are confident it's the only way to expose the truths regarding recent events."

Dick standing at the far right almost between where Cloud sat and the three men brought from jail were seated, explained, "It begins with a man dead in seat 4-A on the flight from Manhattan to Las Vegas."

Dora knew better than to make any comments. Finding the man dead, taking his key and opening the locker in the bus terminal and more, had her lucky the sheriff didn't drag her to police headquarters.

Dick continued, "We know Zachary Kohl died of arsenic poisoning after drinking from the flask he brought with him on the plane. At Jane Kohl's request her housekeeper added it just before his leaving New York. His murder started the chain of events leading to more murders, several attempted murders and finally bringing all of you here to this lovely event tonight."

"Any proof Jane Kohl had him killed?" shouted Benjamin. He knew much of this led right to him.

"Yes. We'll get to that shortly."

"Bull."

"No sir, murder. We also have proof you had a hit out on Jane, to be handled by her husband Zachary. We have the note, cash, gun and photo of her you placed in a bus locker. Problem is once you knew he was dead you attempted to get rid of it all and sent Kody to do your dirty work."

"Bunch of lies." Benjamin was nearly hysterical. He had been caught and he finally knew it. The police officer near him warned him to be quiet.

Kody seemed to be in a state of dead fear, his face white as the proverbial ghost.

"Jane Kohl had photos of you, Benjamin, in an unusual style of dress for a man like yourself, and she was threatening to blackmail you. Unfortunately a young woman working here at The Black Tie walked by when she showed a couple to you. You panicked."

"If he's responsible for all these murders why the hell am I here? I'm leaving."

Deidre got as far as standing up when one of the officers told her, "Sit down or we'll handcuff you, ma'am."

Dick moved on to the next murder.

"Kody was told to go with his pal Gordi to threaten Shannon Flynn. He had also been instructed to kill her and bury her far out of town. Two college boys found her stuffed in an icebox dumped in the desert. Never mind how they got the icebox and took it out there. She was dead is what matters."

Nodding to Faith, she played the tape from Kody to the police saying his father told him to murder her.

Benjamin Rothstein jumped up, went over and smacked his son nearly knocking him off his chair, screaming, "You lying S.O.B."

Sheriff Foster grabbed him and another officer handcuffed him again. It didn't stop him from shouting a barrage of obscenities at his only son.

He quieted down when the sheriff threatened to gag him.

"Well that was delightful," Cloud said, leaning over Zero again to Dora.

Dick walking in the center of the circle, stopping for a minute in front of a couple people then moving on. "I won't go into all the little details making us curious and suspicious. Some things simply didn't make sense."

"Buzz and I followed Kody and Gordi several times out of town to The Underworld Saloon. We also know you've been there often Krupe, you and Jane were having an affair that ended badly in there."

"True, but I never killed anyone. She was a bad lady, asked me to do something to hurt other people. I walked away from her."

"We know." Dick turned and walked over to Gordi. "We also know Gordi was the one who shot at Benjamin at The Black Tie at his request while the Casino Syndicate was having its meeting there. Benjamin hired him to do it and he used blanks."

"He paid me lots of money to do things even helping Kody bury that body in the desert. I needed the money."

Glenn stared at his brother, weary and sad. "He's right. I knew he wanted money for drugs and booze. I had enough, had given him enough. I told my wife there was nothing more I could do to help him. He and Kody both were damaged human beings I felt, beyond help."

"It seems my associates and I were becoming a problem with our following some people, questioning others, and putting ourselves in the middle of murder, blackmail and casino fraud. The sheriff was none too happy with us either, but he forgives us."

Foster glared at him. "Don't push your luck. Get on with this."

"Yes sir. I was about to bring forth the issue of the kidnapping."

Dame Isabella spoke up. "I saw it happen. Then later the fat old man over there in handcuffs tried to kidnap me and hurt me."

Dora saw Dick doing his best not to crack up laughing. "Yes you did, and you've been very brave and helpful."

"I want reward. Zero need to kiss me."

Dick barely controlling himself turned to Zero.

"Sir, would you please reward the lovely lady."

Zero got up, went over and gave Dame Isabella a kiss on each cheek. He returned to his seat, considering how to exact revenge on his pal.

"Back to the kidnapping. Kody and Gordi were responsible for grabbing Cloud and my wife Dora and taking them to The Mob Museum. They bungled it, got caught and were arrested. A dangerous situation was speeding toward some people who decided they needed to find a way to neutralize it."

"What are you talking about? You sound crazy," shouted Deidre.

"She's right, what danger?" one of the two unknown men yelled out.

Dick nodded to Faith who went out into the inner circle by the table and set out the photos of those murdered, Zachary and Shannon, now adding Jane Kohl. "Jane Kohl died a short while ago of gunshot wounds."

Sheriff Foster interjected, "Although an unknown source had already given us copies of photos Jane had taken of Benjamin and a note from her housekeeper saying she asked him to poison her husband, before she died, Jane managed to tell me about the photos she had of Rothstein and proof of their connection to the casino syndicate fraud scheme. She also admitted she had wanted to kill the Zimmermans and shot at their door before rushing off to the airport where she was shot by Benjamin Rothstein."

No one new had been allowed in the room, yet it seemed to become darker, perhaps because Dick was about to become more confrontational, more accusatory toward those who had conspired to do evil for money and power, revenge because of hate.

"Kody, you lied. You wanted to get revenge on your father."

As Glenn Erickson's wife once said about him, "Poor Kody, he never had a chance with that bully of a father."

Dick stood right in front of him. "Look at me. We know your father never told you to murder Shannon Flynn. Someone else did. You also know the two men in here who haven't been introduced. They own The Underworld Saloon and you've spoken to them many times. They paid you for favors and to get information."

Zero whispered to Dora, "He going somewhere big with this?"

Dora nodded.

"The two of you were involved in a plan to discredit Benjamin Rothstein, which was a little crazy when you think about it. He was doing a good job of that himself. He knew those photos could damage the reputation of The Black Tie Hotel and Casino. Kody, you found out about the hit he ordered on Jane Kohl. But Benjamin and Jane weren't the only ones concerned about the Black Tie and what its closing could cost them."

One of the two men stood up, a police officer came over and ordered him to sit down as he shouted across the room, "We're not going to take the blame for this alone."

"Shut up, you damn fool."

Cloud and Zero turned to Dora shocked. "Deidre?"

Chapter Fifty-Eight

Goal: Murder

"**S**he was near us when we were kidnapped and yet they made no attempt to grab her. That didn't make sense. According to a confession from Kody, Deidre wanted them to murder us, not just kidnap us. Hearing the police enter The Mob Museum scared them and that's when they tried to run away."

The private party was over even though the sign was still at the entrance of The Tuxedo Café. Dick and Dora, Cloud and Zero remained. Sheriff Foster, Deputy Turner and half a dozen of Las Vegas' finest had rounded up those accused of various crimes and carted them off to jail. Benjamin was under arrest for the murder of Jane Kohl while his son Kody, along with his pal Gordi, were charged with kidnapping and being complicit in the murder of Shannon Flynn.

The sheriff left with a sly grin and nod to Dick.

Dora was now showing them copies of the articles she had received from Carson about Deidre's family, particularly her father. "She ordered the murder of Shannon Flynn telling Kody to blame his father. The boys grabbed Shannon, took her to Deidre and afterwards came up with the crazy scheme to put her in the icebox and dump it in the desert."

"How did she get them to do what she wanted?" Cloud was fascinated by the whole drama.

"Giving them money, which they used for drugs and alcohol. Deidre's life was based on deception. Her ambitions became complicated by lie upon lie and her life of criminal behavior."

"What made you and Dora suspect Deidre?" Cloud leaned over Zero.

"Dora's intuition. She called our reporter friend in Manhattan and told him she wanted any articles he could find on Deidre Rothstein and her family, suggesting he research her maiden name. That's what did it."

"Did what?" Cloud pressed for more details.

Dora explained, "The articles told about her family and her father's connection to the Mob."

Dick added, "After Dora showed me these articles, I made contact with someone in Manhattan and had him ask a few of his resources some questions we still had. I don't know who they are, don't want to, but I suspect a couple pals from the old days."

"Her father told people he was Mormon, came to Vegas with his three children. When he got here he bought some land, started a small accounting business and said his wife had died. He acted like a straight-laced, conservative type of guy. But…"

"Don't make them beg for the details, darling. I'll get the bartender to bring us some drinks."

"The *but* is her father was from Brooklyn and involved with the Mob. They sent him to Las Vegas because he had finance skills they felt would be beneficial. He couldn't be a made man, you had to be Italian for that distinct honor."

Dick interrupted and continued the story. "He was sent to oversee money laundering operations and extortion, and although never charged it seems he was involved in a few murders, including his wife's. His children grew up being trained to follow in his footsteps. Take over the family business, as he called it."

"What happened to him and his so called family?" Cloud asked, mesmerized by the story.

"His children are Deidre and the two men, both her younger brothers, who own The Underworld Saloon. They used it as a place to get information, listening in to whispered conversations with devices installed under the tables. And they were not against threatening others when necessary. Clearly the new head of the family was Deidre. She was more ruthless, ambitious and hungry. They were fine with her leading the way as long as they got their share of the money coming in from all their criminal activities. And there were plenty over the years. As for the father, many years ago he was found dead in the desert, murdered," Dora said.

Dick asked, "May I take it from here, darling?"

Dora reluctantly nodded.

Dick said, "Deidre set out to trap and manipulate Benjamin Rothstein from the beginning. He needed to expand The Black Tie and she dressed the part to seduce him, had the money to become his partner and eventually his wife. He wanted her money. She wanted the casino as an investment and especially as a cover for whatever else she had in mind. Fortunately for us, the more things began to fall apart, the more out of control she became. And she made some serious mistakes."

A bartender brought a tray of drinks.

"What, no nuts?" asked Zero.

Dick laughed. "Plenty of nuts, just recently left here."

Glenn went home to his wife. "You won't believe this story," he told her.

Krupe left for work in a nearby nightclub.

Buzz drove Dame Isabella home then went to one of his underworld hangouts. He kept shaking his head. "Crazy people."

Deidre left shouting threats and trying to kick the deputy who handcuffed her. Her brothers went quietly, afraid to even look at her.

Zero announced, "Enough. Let's go to dinner."

Cloud stood up and hugged him. "You sure know how to show a lady a good time."

Chapter Fifty-Nine

...And Then...

Ten days after the so-called café party, Zero and Cloud were packed and ready to leave Las Vegas.

"I'm driving Cloud back to Albuquerque although she still refuses to tell me her full name, but I'm working on it, slow and easy, like my love making."

Meanwhile, Dame Isabella sent him a note with kisses that read *I wait for you.*

You had to admire her determination.

"Good grief, Zero, what are you wearing? You look like Tom Mix."

Tipping his tan cowboy hat and showing off new red and black cowboy boots, Zero gave them each a hug goodbye. Cloud did the same, whispering to Dora, "He thinks I don't know he's hoping to convince me to go back to New York with him."

"Will you?"

"I'll be in touch." She smiled.

"By the way, lover boy, revenge is sweet. A little payback for the Dame. I sent a photo of you with your mustache to Bertie. She can't wait to see you." Zero tipped his hat and drove away.

A few days after Zero and Cloud left, Dora said,

"Dick, darling, let's go home."

Meaning Manhattan.

"Think the sheriff will be glad to see us leave?"

"He'll probably send us flowers and champagne," Dora kidded.

Dick called the sheriff to say goodbye.

"Brady, my lovely wife and I are intending to leave your fair city soon. Hope you won't be too sad. Even though you have our taped and signed statements as witnesses, we would be glad to come back for Deidre Rothstein's trial if needed. Anything to be sure she is never allowed to roam the earth free again."

"She's already suggesting an insanity plea. There's certainly an element of insanity to her behavior, but clearly she knew what she was doing. Her brothers, hoping for leniency, are singing like robins in spring. County prosecutors will be happy to send her away for life." Sheriff Brady Foster was a good man dealing with a world of crazies in Las Vegas.

"By the way, Dick, don't take this the wrong way, but I'm delighted to see you and Dora leave. Now I'll only have to deal with normal crazies."

Goodbyes over, Dick let Buzz know his plans. "No problem, Boss. Got some plans of my own."

"You mean drinking and women?"

"Could be, Boss. Could be."

Dora emailed her Manhattan medical examiner friend in New York. *Will be home soon, plan lunch, we had quite a time here. I was kidnapped, there were several murder attempts on Dick and myself and, well, much more to tell you.*

Reading her email response, phone ringing in the background, Dora replied, *Can't wait. I see everything is the same.*

"Dick, answer the phone, dear."

"Dad, it's Jake."

"Are you okay? What's wrong? Are you sick?" Dick, sounding panicked, brought Dora next to him whispering, his hand over the phone, "he sounds upset."

Dora grabbed the phone asking the exact same questions. "Jake, it's Mom, are you okay, what's going on?"

"I'm okay. I'm in the Hamptons with Lily. Her aunt and uncle were found murdered in the historic beach house they inherited. We know the local police are investigating but something is strange. I thought you and Dad could help. Oh and there's a very odd letter from an attorney who told them about the house, saying they needed to come here to handle a transfer of a trust or some such thing."

"Did they meet with the attorney who sent the letter?"

"Well, no one seems to be able to find him."

"Not even the police?"

"No. Mom?"

"Yes."

"There's more. A skeleton was found in the house, dead for over a hundred years, they think. Could you and Dad come? We're not sure what to do."

"No problem, dear. We'll be there soon," Dora said.

The End

Coming Soon...

A Senior Sleuths Mystery Book 3

Featuring Dick and Dora Zimmerman
...With Zero...The Bookie

DEAD IN THAT BEACH HOUSE

by

M. Glenda Rosen

T he windows had been sealed shut, a house unused for nearly a century on land worth a fortune now. The two youths figured out a way to break in, stoned, laughing and within moments stunned into fear. There were three dead bodies. One a century old skeleton on a red velvet dining room chair.

The others, an elderly couple, were on a red velvet sofa.

Dead no longer than a few days.

And a missing attorney for the new owners.

Prologue

The Zimmermans

Zero's girlfriend, Cloud, and I were kidnapped.

We were tied, blindfolded and taken to the basement of The Mob Museum in Las Vegas. Of course we escaped while the confused kidnappers tried to figure out what to do with us. The police knew what to do with them.

I'm Dora Zimmerman. My charming husband Dick and I are retired, sort of. We have a condo in Manhattan and another in Las Vegas. We've been called Senior Sleuths but police chiefs and sheriffs who are less than thrilled with our sleuthing. They've suggested a couple other names for us. We can't help ourselves, murder seems to find us, or even fall into our laps. Literally.

Our long time friend and sleuthing buddy, Zero the Bookie usually joins are adventures. In Vegas, Cloud a Native America woman he met at an online gambling site became part of the adventure. It turned out she worked for the Bureau of Indian Affairs.

Happily they're now enjoying their own affair.

We have other interesting friends and associates, like Frankie Socks in New York who was once in the Witness Protection Program. He keeps an eye on us. He also has connections we feel best not to know about.

Dick and I have been married for 40 years. He used

to be a criminal attorney. He defended a lot of good guys. He also defended some bad guys.

I was a lawyer, then a judge in divorce court. I've said this before there were some criminals there worse than murderers.

Dick and I see our two grown sons a few times a year. They love us. Mostly from a distance since they think we get into too much trouble.

It changed when we recently got a call from our son Jake. His girlfriend's aunt and uncle were murdered.

Jake and Lily had gone to the Hamptons to meet them. They inherited a 100 year old home in a part of the country where it was clearly worth a great deal of money.

"Lily we don't know about will and lawyers and stuff. Could you come and help us, please?"

Uncle Willie Sinclair knew she wouldn't be able to refuse him. They were family and they knew a thing or two about each others' past.

After Jake called us we immediately made plans to fly east, by-passing Manhattan, the city we dearly love, landing on the suburban crawl of Long Island, where Frankie Socks met us in a rented town car and drove us to the Hamptons.

The Hamptons has become mostly posh and pretentious thanks to big money and big egos. There amongst the rich and famous and wannabe' we found ourselves involved in more than one mystery of lies, greed, contempt for the law and murders.

Well dear friend here is where our next sleuthing adventure took place and oh yes, there was certainly more than one murder.

The first one, "Dead in Bed," was exciting, well

except for when the bad guys tried to kill us. The second, "Dead in Seat 4-A, as I said, had us being kidnapped, involved in a couple more murders and being chased around The Mob Museum by what looked like the three stooges.

I thought it all exciting. Dick not so much.

In the Hamptons, where the land and ocean and sky are filled with beauty we encountered ugly secrets, excessive greed, deceit, revenge and of course the forementioned murders.

We also became involved in a disturbing world where the elderly were romanced, others tricked out of their money and all too many were abused and even murdered.

And then there was the lunatic obsessed with Sherlock Holmes.

By the way, you know I do love Dick to death.

Chapter One

Jake (Jacob) Zimmerman

"I 'm calling my parents."

"Why?"

"They're sort of known for solving murders."

"Sort of? What are they, detectives?"

"Not exactly."

"Okay, what exactly?"

Jake Zimmerman was telling his girlfriend and business partner about his mother and father, and what they sort of did.

"My mother is a retired judge, my father a retired attorney, their best friend Zero is not a retired bookie. They seem to have an uncanny ability to help solve crimes, especially murders."

"You think they really can find out what happened to my aunt and uncle?"

"Maybe."

Lily had met his parents briefly one time, over a year ago. She didn't know much about his family and friends. Jake wasn't sure he did either. Oh, he knew Zero, he was like an uncle to him, he met some others at his parents' fortieth wedding anniversary party a few years back, a strange mix of people from when they worked, organizations they had belonged to and supported, and some that looked like they hoodlums, tough guys you wouldn't want to meet alone in a dark alley at night.

"Are these all your friends?" he recalled asking his dad.

"Sure, from different times in our lives, now and in the past." Dick had grinned, put his arm around Jake and steered him to the bar where the party was held in a beautiful room at the Waldorf Hotel in Manhattan.

"What about the guy standing alone in the corner?"

"Him? Oh, he recently got out of the witness protection program." With that Jake downed a scotch and soda and ordered another.

"My folks have interesting friends who help them from time to time. I don't know much more than that, I've been told it's best I don't know. I agree."

There was the charming Zimmerman smile, like his father and his grandfather, Jacob Zimmerman, who he was named after. Jake was good looking, tall, lean and to be truthful much more like his mother, who had the greater sense of adventure and the determined mindset to dig deep into a mystery.

Since he was in pre-school, his sense of adventure led him to be known as a handful. In truth that began when he found a way to open the school gate and let all the children out onto the busy street.

The school politely and firmly informed Jake's parents that private school would be best for him.

Age four and expelled for pre-school.

His mother loved it. All these years later, her son almost forty, and thinking about it made her grin.

Jake and Lily were a couple, they would agree, still

they kept their own apartments. Jake did not have marriage on his mind.

Not at all.

Lily hoped one day that would change.

The murder of her aunt and uncle would bring to light a lot more about her story than she had ever told Jake.

Some family stories should be left behind the cloud of secrecy, keeping curious intruders away. There are life and death stories in all families.

But are they by natural causes? Or murder?

To Be Continued....

Acknowledgements

So many thanks to my wonderful editors, Verena Rose and Shawn Reilly Simmons, for the essential final edits of the book, and Michelle Perin-Callahan who helped me with editing through the development phase.

And finally, with great, continued appreciation to my publisher, Level Best Books, for giving voice to my mysterious mind.

Marcia

A Note From the Author

None of us are innocent. We all keep secrets about who we are and things we know. In my case, I have been able to put these past family peccadilloes and experiences to use. No doubt, thanks to my father, writing mysteries is in my DNA!

MYSTERY SCENE MAGAZINE 154

Although you might think it strange, I suggest you ask yourself what your motivation is for writing or wanting to write mysteries. In *The Senior Sleuths*, the actions of my senior characters, Dick and Dora, often reflect my truths about life and relationships.

WOMAN'S NATIONAL BOOK ASSOCIATION/SAN FRANCISCO

M. Glenda Rosen has previously published four books in her *Dying to Be Beautiful* mystery series. Rosen is also author of *The Woman's Business Therapist* and award winning *My Memoir Workbook*. She was founder and owner of a successful marketing and public relations agency for many years and received numerous awards for her work with business and professional women. She is a member of several mystery writer's organizations and The Mob Museum in Las Vegas. She currently resides in Carmel, California.

Made in the USA
Columbia, SC
07 February 2019